*"Kendall? D[...]
any of your [dream?]*

Taking a deep breath, Kendall tried to figure out what she should say, but her mind was still filled with images of her body entwined with Jared's. She had to tell him something. "I...uh...only images, really. There was a big grassy area and a pond. It was fuzzy looking."

At least all of that was true.

"Okay. What were you doing?" Jared continued.

Please don't ask me any more questions, she thought. Not even for the sake of science would Kendall tell Jared what had really happened in that dream. And she didn't think she would ever have to worry about forgetting it, either, for the images were burned into her memory.

"Do you remember anything else?"

Like the fact that I was naked and you were naked and we were about to make love and it was fantastic? "No, nothing really."

Dear Reader,

October is a very special month at Silhouette Romance. We're celebrating the most precious love of all . . . a child's love. Our editors have selected five heartwarming stories that feature happy-ever-afters with a family touch—*Home for Thanksgiving* by Suzanne Carey, *And Daddy Makes Three* by Anne Peters, *Casey's Flyboy* by Vivian Leiber, *Paper Marriage* by Judith Bowen and *Beloved Stranger* by Peggy Webb.

But that's not all! We're also continuing our WRITTEN IN THE STARS series. This month we're proud to present one of the most romantic heroes in the zodiac—the Libra man—in Patricia Ellis's *Pillow Talk*.

I hope you enjoy this month's stories, and in the months to come, watch for Silhouette Romance novels by your all-time favorites, including Diana Palmer, Brittany Young, Annette Broadrick and many others.

The authors and editors of Silhouette Romance books strive to bring you the best of romance fiction, stories that capture the laughter, the tears—the sheer joy—of falling in love. Let us know if we've succeeded. We'd love to hear from you!

Happy Reading,

Valerie Susan Hayward
Senior Editor

PATRICIA ELLIS

Pillow Talk

Silhouette Romance

Published by Silhouette Books New York

America's Publisher of Contemporary Romance

SILHOUETTE BOOKS
300 E. 42nd St., New York, N.Y. 10017

PILLOW TALK

ISBN: 0-373-08820-5

First Silhouette Books printing October 1991

Books by Patricia Ellis

Silhouette Romance

Sweet Protector #684
Champagne and Wildflowers #799
Pillow Talk #820

PATRICIA ELLIS

was "dramatized" at a very young age and never recovered. After a life spent in and out of institutions... of higher education, she now holds two degrees in theater arts, and she acts whenever she's allowed, which is never often enough. A stubborn believer in happy endings, it was predictable that this optimist, who loves Shakespearean comedy (but is constantly trying to find a way to help Romeo and Juliet out of that mess they're in), would fall under the spell of romance novels. Several years later, between theater degrees, she decided to try writing one of her favorite kinds of books. Imagine her delight when an obviously brilliant and perspicacious editor at Silhouette bought that book. Imagine a standing ovation on opening night, and you've got the picture. Now, writing and acting may not be the most secure professions to pursue, but—hands down—they're the most creatively fulfilling. Not to mention the most fun.

A Note from the Author

Dear Reader,

Always fascinated by the unusual and the unexpected, I was immediately charmed by the idea of writing the Libra book for the WRITTEN IN THE STARS series.

Doing research at my local bookstore was no great chore . . . especially since I work there part-time. But as I lost myself in cardinal signs and ruling planets, my only slightly wandering gaze fell upon some nearby books on dreams and dreaming. Hmm . . . what if . . . ?

What if . . . Those two simple yet magical words set me on the paper trail that was to become *Pillow Talk*. It wasn't a particularly arduous journey, but it was an endlessly fascinating one.

I've always been a fair-weather fan of astrology and knew that I could pass off my pack-rat tendencies and overweening sentimentality on the fact that I was a Cancer. But after learning more about cardinal and water signs, I find that I have even more excuses for my sometimes unpredictable personality.

And since I keep my own dream journal anyway, it seemed natural for me to combine these two somewhat unconventional interests into a romance about two people who happened to share those interests. I got them together, but after that, Jared and Kendall were on their own. I think they did all right for themselves.

Sincerely,

Patricia Ellis

Chapter One

"There she goes again. That's number six. And it's only three-thirty."

Looking over at the television monitor in question, he scanned the image of the sleeping woman. "Mrs. Donlevy keeps herself busy at night."

"But, Jared," the younger man said softly, "she never remembers any of them."

"She will, Larry," Jared told him, his dark brown eyes calmly assured. "This is only her second session."

"Right."

A few minutes later Mrs. Donlevy grunted and opened her eyes. Larry leaned forward and pressed a switch.

"Mrs. Donlevy? Do you remember any of the dream you just had?"

The woman lay there for a moment, then cleared her throat. "Yes, I do. I was at the beach, sitting in my lounge chair. George and I were arguing about where to put the umbrella. Finally we both got settled and I got comfort-

able with my book. Suddenly I started sinking into the
sand. I mean the whole lounge chair! Even the umbrella
was sinking. Everything around me was going under, except for my husband. I couldn't get out and no one on the
beach seemed to notice. I tried to yell for my husband, but
George was asleep in his lounge chair and wouldn't wake
up. Just as I sank under the sand, I woke up.''

Larry made some notes, then pressed the switch again.
''Thank you, Mrs. Donlevy. It's only three forty-five now,
so you can go back to sleep.''

''But what did that dream mean?''

Larry looked at Jared, who shook his head. Larry
pressed the switch once more. ''We aren't interpreting
dreams in this study, Mrs. Donlevy. We're mainly interested in how and why we dream.''

''Oh. Well, never mind, because I think I know what it
means, and George is going to have to answer to me.''

Larry didn't respond. Instead he looked at Jared. ''That
woman is going to drive me nuts before this experiment is
over.''

''All part of the process, Larry. And it isn't a good idea
to use the term 'nuts' in this building.''

''Sure. So, what do you think so far? I mean, is this
project going the way you want it to?''

Leaning back in his chair, Jared frowned. ''It's hard to
tell yet, but I suppose it is. There does seem to be something missing, although I haven't put my finger on it yet.''

''Excitement,'' Larry declared. ''That's what's missing.''

Jared chuckled. ''If you wanted excitement, you
shouldn't have signed on with me for this study.''

''What? And miss the chance to work with you and
further my own selfish interests? You're the closest thing

to famous this department has. Besides, I live with the hope that something unpredictable will happen.''

Nodding thoughtfully, Jared said, ''Maybe it will.''

What Jared didn't say was that, he too, was disappointed by the lack of spark in the subjects so far. Only a couple of them looked promising at all, although it really was too early to tell. But if things didn't change soon, he was afraid this whole experiment might have to be redone at a later date with different subjects. And if that one didn't work, the project wouldn't retain its funding. After having spent a year of his life so far on the research, Jared put that thought firmly aside. This project was his baby and it would be successful. Just like everything else he did.

''What's up with this faculty meeting this afternoon?''

Jared blinked at his assistant. ''What meeting?''

''Doc, don't you ever read the departmental memos Millie sends down here?''

''Why should I, when I have you to read them for me?''

Larry shrugged. ''Gotta keep up on the doings of the department. Anyway, there's a special faculty meeting this afternoon at five.''

''Five? I won't be up yet.''

''I'm betting Millie will get you up. It's mandatory.''

Jared frowned and looked back at the monitors. ''I wonder what's so important?''

''If you don't know and I don't know,'' Larry announced, ''no one knows. And I'll bet it's driving them all nuts.''

''Please, Larry, we're *psychologists*,'' Jared protested, his lips quirking into a grin.

''Right. Then I'll bet it's driving them all . . . to distraction.''

''What's up, Millie? We know you know.''

The secretary calmly looked up at the two young women

standing in front of her and tried to appear stern. The fact
that she failed didn't seem to daunt her. "I just typed the
memo—I don't know what the meeting is about. And even
if I did know, I couldn't tell you. You should know that,
Dr. Munson. So should you by now, Dr. Arden."

"Oh, don't get all formal on us, Millie." Chloe Munson sighed. "Kendall and I just want to know what to expect from this surprise faculty meeting this afternoon."

"That's right, Millie. And if it's bad news—like a
budget cut—we want to be prepared," Kendall added, a
worried frown marring the smoothness of her brow. "Especially me, since I'm likely to be the first to go—I was the
last to be hired."

Millie's warm heart couldn't stand it. "Oh, all right."
She leaned forward and said conspiratorially, "I can tell
you that it isn't bad news. No budget cuts and no one's
getting the ax. It's good news. Very good news, in fact.
Now go away, I have work to do."

Their curiosity may not have been fully satisfied, but
Kendall and Chloe left and headed down the hall to the
office they had shared for the past six months, ever since
Kendall had begun teaching in the psychology department at Chesapeake State University.

"At least we know it isn't bad news." Chloe smiled as
she opened the door to their office and went in. "But what
in the world could the good news be? There hasn't been
one word of gossip about this, so it had to have happened
just recently."

Kendall dropped her book bag on her desk and sank into
the chair. "I don't care what it is. Just as long as I know I
have a job come September."

"I told you that budget cuts are never surprises."

Nodding, Kendall tucked a strand of chin-length strawberry-blond hair behind one ear and looked at her friend, office mate and roommate. "I know. But I was lucky to get this job and I really love working here. I guess I just keep worrying that something is going to go wrong."

Chloe's smile was understanding. "What happened at your last job was an isolated incident. Everybody likes you here at CSU and I'm sure you'll get tenure soon."

"Not if I don't get something published, I won't," Kendall stated. Pulling a file from the cabinet next to her desk, she laid it on her desk and opened it. "But if I can get this project successfully finished and the paper on it written, I'm sure I can get it published. I've already had a response from a publisher on one query letter. If the experiment is successful and I can prove my theory, they're definitely interested."

"But can you?" Chloe asked. "I mean, can you prove that astrological traits can be matched accurately and used in clinical psychology casework?"

Kendall picked up a pen and tapped it on the surface of her blotter. "If I didn't think that the theory had merit, I wouldn't be doing this project. There is quite a bit of consistency in astrological-trait theories and I think that they can be applied in casework to help identify behavioral patterns and abnormalities."

"Just so you know that the scientific community isn't likely to offer you any words of encouragement."

Kendall shrugged. "I know that the vast majority of psychologists think that astrology is nonsense, but that's where the challenge is. It wasn't so long ago that nobody believed in ESP, either. And now it's an accepted and studied phenomenon."

"I'm willing to keep an open mind about it," Chloe offered. "But I don't think many of the professors in this department would. As you've probably surmised by now, for the most part they're a conservative bunch. The only person, other than myself, who might be on your side would be Jared Dalton, and that's only because he works on aspects of psychology that are not in the least conservative. Most of the old guys are still suspicious of him.''

"But he's been successful," Kendall argued. "He's respected.''

"And he's incredibly good-looking."

Kendall had been thinking exactly the same thing and her gray eyes suddenly shot over to meet Chloe's knowing smirk. "What has that got to do with anything?''

"Not a thing to me," Chloe said airily, "since I'm engaged to my own incredibly good-looking man. You, on the other hand, have a thing for him.''

"I do not," Kendall denied, feeling her cheeks grow warm at the lie. "I don't even know him.''

Chloe laughed. "Kendall, it's okay. So you have a crush on the fantastic Dr. Dalton. So do half the women on staff in the department and most of the girls in his classes.''

"Crushes are for adolescents," Kendall mumbled, trying to read some notes she'd just written.

"Don't be ridiculous. Crushes are for anyone. Of course, if you'd like it to be more than a crush, you'll have to stop hiding from him and let him know you're interested.''

Her pretend interest in her notes was forgotten as Kendall shook her head at Chloe. "No. Regardless of how great he looks, I wouldn't want to go out with him. Even if he asked me, which he wouldn't, I wouldn't go.''

"You wouldn't?''

"I don't date men I work with.''

"Just because you had a problem with a coworker at your last job doesn't mean—''

"I don't date coworkers," Kendall restated. "There are too many complications when the parties involved break up. The strain on a working relationship can be too great. And right now my job is more important to me than the prospect of a few dates with any man—including Jared Dalton. Any thoughts I entertain about Jared are going to remain . . . thoughts and nothing more."

Chloe caught Kendall's hesitation and pounced. "You haven't dreamed about him by any chance, have you?"

When Kendall was slow in answering, Chloe leaned forward, her brown eyes huge. "You *have,* haven't you? Why didn't you tell me? What if it comes true? What was it about?"

Kendall covered her face with her hands. "All right, I've dreamed about him. I didn't tell you because it's stupid and it isn't going to come true."

"How can you say that? You dreamed about our cat— Boris. And you dreamed that I would be getting married right after we became roommates—before I even met Brice. If our cat and my fiancé don't count as realized premonitions, then what does?"

"Very little of what I dream becomes reality, Chloe," Kendall told her friend, not for the first time. "I don't even remember most of them."

"I think you should talk to Jared about your abilities. He's been doing research on sleep and dreaming for over a year."

Kendall's head shook vigorously. "No. I don't want to be prodded and questioned and tested. My parents had me checked out when I was little and the doctors told them I was making it all up."

"But so much has happened in the field since then," Chloe reasoned.

"No," Kendall said.

Chloe glanced at her watch and rose. "I'd love to stay and argue the point with you, but I have a class in five minutes. I'll see you this afternoon at the meeting."

Kendall nodded and watched as Chloe left. Chloe may have been a wonderful teacher and child psychologist, but Kendall wasn't about to be talked out of her position on the subject of her dreams. She didn't want her dreams exposed for scrutiny, and she had very good reasons for keeping working relationships separate from romantic relationships. But she didn't want to dwell on them now.

Returning to her notes, she focused her concentration on her research project. Astrology might not be an accepted science to the psychological community in general, but Kendall hoped that her experiment would at least cause a few of them to think twice about it.

The rest of the day seemed to drag on in an exasperatingly snaillike manner. Following her two morning classes, Kendall had a lunch break, an office hour, and then taught the lab portion of her Introductory Psychology class. After that she had another hour to cool her heels before the departmental meeting was scheduled.

Going into the empty lecture room early, Kendall chose a seat off to one side and toward the back. She pulled a book from her bag and made a pretense of reading it, but realized she wasn't comprehending much when other people started wandering into the room a few minutes later.

Hearing snatches of the quiet conversations around her, Kendall gave up all thoughts of reading and shamelessly eavesdropped. She was disappointed not to hear anything more than she already knew. Theories were being bandied about, but no one really knew anything, and everyone was apprehensive about what was to happen.

Putting her book back into her bag, Kendall looked around the room, noting that almost everyone was present except Chloe and Millie. Jared Dalton was not in the room, either.

Kendall grimaced to think of it, but she hadn't needed to look to know that Dr. Dalton wasn't around. Ever since she'd first laid eyes on the man, his mere presence in a room was enough to cause the hairs on her neck to rise annoyingly. Awareness of a man was one thing, Kendall thought, but this had gone on too long.

She had just decided to marshal her inner resources and banish this stupid crush from her mind when the hairs on the back of her neck stood up and awareness crackled through her. Groaning inwardly at her adolescent reactions, Kendall nevertheless looked over her right shoulder, and sure enough, there he was, looking irritable.

Millie was right behind him, and she looked harried. No doubt she'd had to drag Dr. Dalton out of his lab—or perhaps out of bed. Kendall knew that Jared slept during the day because he conducted his experiments at night in his lab.

He was a little disheveled and Kendall thought that maybe she'd been right—he had just gotten out of bed and rushed over here against his will. The thought of Jared Dalton in bed was definitely worth a few minutes of contemplation, Kendall thought before she could stop herself.

He was probably a swimmer, she guessed, noting his narrow hips and widening torso and shoulders. As her eyes lingered on the breadth of his shoulders beneath the fabric of his shirt, Kendall wondered if his body was really as hard and muscular as it seemed. She wondered if he had hair on his chest. . . .

Her eyes moved back upward, over his Adam's apple
and to that sexy dimple in his chin. His lips were perfect—
sensual, but not too full. His nose was aquiline, and his
eyes were deep brown and... *staring straight into hers!*

Horrified at having been caught, Kendall jerked herself
around to face forward, her cheeks flaming with embarrassment. Adding to her discomfort was the fact that the
expression in his eyes had been amusement mixed with
puzzlement. He was, no doubt, trying to remember her
name, she thought ruefully.

Hearing someone take the seat directly behind her,
Kendall closed her eyes. It was him. Hadn't he embarrassed her enough? If Chloe hadn't chosen that exact moment to sit down beside her, Kendall would have moved.
Instead she sat there, intensely aware of the man who sat
only a couple of feet away, wearing some sinfully aro-
matic cologne.

The head of the department, Dr. Grady, came in and
signaled for quiet. "Thank you all for coming on such
short notice," he said. "I know that you're all wondering
what has happened, and I have to tell you that it was only
a few days ago that I was informed. But I must say, it is
extremely good news. Not only for one of you, but for the
whole department, indeed, the whole university."

Chloe leaned toward Kendall. "I haven't seen old Grady
this excited since he was asked to appear on a panel of
psychologists on TV two years ago."

"I was informed by the dean of the college of arts and
sciences," Dr. Grady continued, "that the will of Everett
Gundersson, professor emeritus of this department, had
cleared probate and that Dr. Gundersson had set up a fund
to be used for faculty research."

His words set the room to buzzing as everyone talked
amongst themselves. Chloe again leaned toward Kendall.

"Gundersson was a funny old guy. His family had left him all kinds of money, but it never seemed as though he was interested in it. Of course, he had already retired when I came here three years ago, but everyone thought the world of him."

Dr. Grady continued to speak despite the soft whispering that never completely died out. "Also stipulated in his will was that every two years, starting with this year, an award be given to the faculty member whose ongoing research enhances not only the study of psychology, but whose innovation and dedication bring the attention of laymen and scientists alike to CSU.

"So, to that end, on June the first of this year, the first award of $25,000 will be granted to the faculty member whose research the award committee feels most deserving of Dr. Gundersson's gift."

That stopped the whispers. A dead silence fell over the room for the space of several seconds. Then applause and loud questions erupted.

Kendall sat benumbed. *Twenty-five thousand dollars.* With that kind of money she could mount a fantastic experiment to expand on her theories of astrological traits. But then she remembered that it was doubtful that any committee would grant the award to someone researching astrology.

Apparently everyone else had a question or a comment. Dr. Grady signaled for silence. "Yes, it is very exciting news, and I know you all have questions. But I really would rather have you read the report I've written with the help of the executor of Dr. Gundersson's will before starting with the questions."

Millie began passing out the reports. Kendall took hers and flipped through it absently, noting that it was only about ten pages long. She planned to read it carefully as soon as the meeting was over.

"Please read this and then talk to me. The main thing you should remember is that the award is for *research in progress*. So only those of you currently involved in a project would be eligible this year. The rest of you might want to start thinking about the next prize, to be awarded year after next."

With that he stepped away from the podium and tried to make his way out of the room, but he was stopped four or five times by different people. Kendall rose slowly and noted absently that Jared was gone. Chloe walked out of the room ahead of her and they made their way to their office.

"Twenty-five grand," Chloe sighed as they gathered their things and prepared to leave. "With that kind of money I could open a clinic."

Kendall nodded. Chloe had been working on a project to examine the use of art therapy in child psychology. She had been trying, without much success, to raise money for a facility in Baltimore.

"We could all use that kind of money," Kendall agreed.

They left the office and then the building, still contemplating what would be a boon for the person who won the grant.

"You know," Chloe said as they walked the few short blocks to the rented house they shared, "there aren't that many people in the department with current projects. You and me, of course. Kevin Carlson is working on primate communication in conjunction with the anthropology and zoology departments. And Dr. Sawcicki has been working on a theory of behavior modification in laboratory rats for ages. By now most of the rats are just pets of his. And I'd hardly call his work innovative anymore."

"I don't think that the rest of us have much to worry about," Kendall said as she walked up the front steps of their house and unlocked the door.

"What do you mean?" Chloe asked as they went in.

"I mean that Jared Dalton is going to get the award."

Chloe dropped her book bag on the floor and flopped onto the sofa. "Oh, yeah. Jared."

A huge gray cat jumped onto the sofa and marched over Chloe's arms until she began stroking him.

Kendall put her own bag on the coffee table and sat in an armchair, which had the same blue print as the sofa. "Jared already has a solid reputation in the field—he's had several articles published and this fall a textbook he wrote is coming out. On top of that is the project on sleep and dreaming he's working on. There's no way he won't win."

Chloe frowned. "How did you find out so much about Jared?"

Kendall's left eyebrow arched sardonically. "How could I not? You aren't the only one who talks about him, you know. So does everyone else in the department."

"Of course," Chloe allowed. "But I don't think we should just give up. Jared's current experiment has raised a lot of stuffed shirts' eyebrows over the past year or so. As with astrology, not everyone is as open-minded about the study of dreams as we are."

Kendall considered this. "That's true. Although, if a committee is skeptical about his project, they'll laugh me right out the door."

"Not if you've proved your theory," Chloe argued, "and if Jared's findings are inconclusive. Besides, until the grant is awarded, everyone has an equal chance. And I, for one, am going to apply for it."

"I hope this doesn't mean that you won't be able to participate in my project as a test subject," Kendall said hesitantly.

Chloe shook her fist at her roommate. "Don't be a jerk. Of course I'll still be in your project. Just because we'll both be working on grant projects doesn't mean we can't help each other out. I'd have you helping me except that you aren't a disturbed child."

Kendall groaned. "No, I'm only a disturbed adult. Well, if you're going to go ahead and apply for the grant, then so am I. And may the best project win."

"That's the attitude. Positive thinking is the way to positive results."

Sinking lower in her chair, Kendall found her bright outlook darkening by the second. "Unfortunately, unless I can find another subject as willing as you to learn enough about astrological traits to identify and predict behavior patterns, then my application won't get past the committee's first screening, much less win."

"Have you asked everybody?"

"They all said no. Most of them also laughed."

"Everyone?" Chloe pressed.

Kendall frowned. "Everyone..." Finally understanding what Chloe meant, Kendall set her jaw. "Practically everyone."

Chloe shoved Boris away, then stretched out on her stomach, facing Kendall. "I didn't say you had to go out with him, Kendall, but you should at least be able to work with the man. It isn't as if you don't get along. You barely even know him."

"Maybe I'll try someone in the sociology department," Kendall mused.

Chloe groaned in frustration. "All right, be a stubborn mule, but don't complain to me anymore about there being no one else who will help you."

"He probably wouldn't do it, either," Kendall said.

"But you won't know that for sure until you ask him, will you?"

Watching Chloe as she left the room, Kendall knew that her roommate was right and that she should have asked Jared when she asked all her other colleagues if they would be willing to participate in her project.

She simply hadn't been willing to confront him. He was never around like so many of the others were, for one thing. All the other faculty members could be found at one time or another in the faculty lounge on the third floor of the psych building. Not Jared Dalton. As far as Kendall knew, he spent all of his time in his lab and in his classes.

The only times she'd seen him were at the weekly faculty meetings and occasionally as he raced by in the hallway. And she had wished from the moment she'd met him at the faculty cocktail party in September that one of them hadn't been working in the psychology department.

Kendall had never been so immediately or so totally attracted to a man in her life. At first it had been his looks. Next it was the sound of his deep voice when he answered some question put to him. Then she came to recognize his after-shave....

But regardless of her attraction to him, she was determined not to acknowledge it. Dating a coworker had spelled disaster for her at her last position, and Kendall had vowed that it wasn't going to happen at CSU.

Boris, abandoned by Chloe, decided that Kendall might as well do patting duty, and he leapt from the sofa to the chair and into her lap.

"Well, hello, Boris. Sure, I'll pat you. It's easier than trying to come up with a solution to my own problems."

The next morning Kendall wasn't any closer to solving her problem than she had been the night before. Except that now she was actually considering asking Jared Dalton for his help.

Chloe, as she was quick to remind Kendall, was right. If she intended to work in the same building every day with Jared for the next twenty or thirty years, then she had better get over her silly crush and develop a professional attitude.

And that was exactly the pep talk Kendall gave herself as she entered the departmental office and asked Millie for Jared's office hours.

"Got desperate, did you?"

Millie's shrewd question brought a wry smile to Kendall's lips. "How'd you guess?"

"Because no one asks for his office hours, and I know you've been scouring the department for another subject. If you ask me, they're all being close-minded. I like reading my horoscope and I think astrology is interesting."

"Thanks, Millie," Kendall said. "I appreciate that. Lately, all I've gotten are smirks and laughs."

"I know. And I hate to tell you, but I doubt that Jared Dalton is going to be much better. He's not as conservative as the rest of them, but he is skeptical of anything that can't be scientifically proven."

Even though she had feared as much, Kendall still felt depressed by Millie's words. "I can't say that I'm surprised, given the reactions of the rest of the faculty."

"Well, now, that doesn't mean he won't do it," Millie said. "He isn't a very predictable man, you know."

"Actually I don't know," Kendall admitted.

"Oh, that's right." Millie grinned. "You've only been here since September."

Chloe entered the office then and went to check her mailbox. Seeing Kendall talking to Millie, she went over and leaned one hip against the desk.

"Well, have you decided to ask him?"

"She asked for his office hours," Millie answered.

Chloe smiled. "That's a step in the right direction."

"But then I had to go and tell her that he was skeptical of things he couldn't prove, and now I don't know what she's going to do."

"Kendall, you aren't going to back out, are you?"

Looking from Chloe to Millie, Kendall laughed. "I guess I can't since the two of you are counting on me so much." The other two women laughed with her.

They were still chuckling when Jared Dalton breezed through the doorway. He stopped in front of Millie's desk, next to Kendall.

"A good joke," he asked, his deep voice rasping along Kendall's nerve endings. "Or are you all suffering from an interesting psychosis?"

"Neither," Millie managed. "Did you get up on the wrong side of the bed this morning? Oh, never mind, you couldn't have done that, since you haven't gone to bed yet. What are you doing here? Don't you usually leave by nine?"

Jared frowned and looked at his watch. "Yes, I do. And I would like to go home and get some sleep. But I had an early appointment today with one of my subjects, and she hasn't shown. Could you find Lizbeth Shaw's phone number and call her to see where she is?"

"Oh, I put a message in your mailbox a few minutes ago. I think it was from her."

Jared moved over to the wooden cubbyholes that served as mailboxes and removed several messages. He picked up the top one and unfolded it.

Millie, in the meantime, was motioning with her head that Kendall should make her move. Chloe was also making pointed gestures. Kendall was decidedly reluctant. She didn't want an audience while she made her pitch. It would be difficult enough when he turned her down if she was alone, but people watching would make it worse.

"She quit!"

All three women jumped at the sound of Jared's shout. They turned to look at him and Millie nodded. "Yes. I think she said something about quitting because her boyfriend was joining the navy. She's going to join up, too. Then they're getting married."

"Isn't that sweet?" Chloe purred.

Jared just scowled. "Very romantic, I'm sure. But couldn't she have waited until my experiment is over at the end of the semester? I knew I shouldn't have used a student, but it seems that the only people in that age range in this town are all students here. Now I'll have to replace her."

"That's too bad," Millie sympathized. "But your actual experiments only began last week, didn't they? I'm sure you'll get someone quickly. By the way," she added innocuously, "Dr. Arden here wanted to speak with you about something. And since you apparently have some free time..."

Kendall glared at Millie, but the secretary had turned to her work and begun typing furiously. Looking away from the secretary, Kendall found herself being regarded curiously by Jared. If he'd been old and ugly, she thought, this whole thing would be a lot easier. Jared then looked at his watch again.

"Right. Well, since I've been stood up by an ungrateful WAVE and you're already here, why don't we go down to my office?"

"Uh, I, that's all right," Kendall stammered. "It can wait. I know you probably want to go home and—"

"Actually, Jared," Chloe interrupted, "you and Kendall both have problems and I think you could help each other out."

"Chloe," Kendall warned, "I don't think that Jared is... What do you mean, help each other out?"

Staring at her roommate's inane smile, Kendall had no idea what Chloe was up to, but she was fairly sure she didn't want to hear it.

But apparently Jared did.

"And how could we do that?" he said.

"Simple," Chloe elaborated. "You need a subject for your project, and Kendall needs a subject for her project. You help her and she'll help you and everybody is happy, right?"

Kendall thought that she just might have one less roommate by morning.

Chapter Two

Standing in Jared's office a few minutes later, Kendall was furiously trying to signal Chloe to shut up. But Chloe was on a roll, and she just smiled at Kendall and kept going.

"Now, Dr. Arlen," Jared said when Chloe paused for breath, "what is it that Chloe is talking about? How can we help each other?"

Feeling out of her depth, Kendall fought for some professional composure. If she was going to have to go through with this farce, at the very least, she was going to make sure he knew who she was.

"Actually, my name is Arden. Kendall Arden. And I may have a doctorate, but I'd rather be called Kendall."

"All right." Jared smiled at her.

When Kendall then just stared at him, Chloe cleared her throat. "It's February, Jared. Kendall has been here since September. Surely you've met by now."

"Of course, we have," Jared agreed. "But it was at the beginning of the semester at one of those faculty cocktail parties, I'm sure."

He was not only sure, Kendall thought, but precisely accurate. They had met at that function. He had been hustled off by the dean, and Kendall had spent most of the evening getting to know Chloe, who had been in need of a roommate at the time. Kendall hadn't thought he'd remembered her at all from that night.

"It doesn't really matter," Kendall managed to say.

"You're always at the faculty meetings," he said with a frown. "But we've never actually spoken outside of that."

"Maybe she's shy," Chloe quipped.

"Maybe I just haven't had anything to say yet," Kendall said to Chloe.

"Anyway, I know who you are." Jared chuckled. "I'm just not very good with names. I'm sorry. You teach a couple of intro classes, don't you? And a developmental class, right?"

Kendall blinked up at him. "Right."

"You needn't look so surprised. I work here, too. I like to think I know what's going on around me."

Chloe laughed. "Some of us have had our doubts about you."

He ignored Chloe and spoke to Kendall. "So, tell me why you needed to talk to me."

Refusing to look at Chloe, Kendall kept her gaze steady on Jared's expectant expression and said, "It's for the project I'm working on. I need another professor to agree to be trained using a method of evaluation I've developed."

Nodding in understanding, Jared sat on the edge of his desk and gestured for them to sit. Chloe chose a comfortable chair in the corner next to a file cabinet. Kendall shook her head. She was too nervous to sit.

"I take it that no one else was willing to help you out?"

Kendall was nodding when she heard Chloe clearing her throat. "Oh, right. Chloe is helping me out. But I need two subjects. And everyone else expressed, shall we say, doubts about my theory. In fact, I'm surprised you haven't already heard about it."

"I've been rather busy the past few months," Jared explained. "But I am intrigued. What's so taboo that my esteemed colleagues have refused to help?"

Kendall took a deep breath and said, "It's a study of the feasibility of using astrological-sign traits to predict behavior in clinical psychology." Then she waited.

His dark eyes narrowed and then he looked away. He was going to make fun of her, Kendall decided.

"What made you decide to research something like astrology?" he asked.

At least he hadn't laughed at her, she reasoned. Skepticism she could handle. "Astrology is so ancient that I've always wondered how something that has survived so many hundreds of years could be totally ignored. Scientifically, that is," she said carefully. "Although there are legions of charlatans out there, I was curious about how accurate astrological personality traits are. I wanted to know if astrology could be used as an aid—a supplement—in casework."

He nodded, but Kendall couldn't tell if it was because he was considering her words seriously, or if he was thinking she was wacky.

"I should tell you, Kendall, that I don't put much stock in the so-called 'science' of astrology."

She wasn't surprised. "I expected as much. And though I don't really expect you to agree with the theory of astrology, I would hope for a little latitude as far as my investigation of the subject is concerned. I'm including a statistical survey of at least a hundred randomly chosen people in my paper. I hope to demonstrate that someone besides me—Chloe and, I hope, you, in this case—can identify a person's astrological sign by studying their self-ascribed personality traits. And, conversely, could help identify personality problems by using a patient's astrological-trait chart."

Jared nodded again. He didn't look convinced, but he wasn't laughing at her, either.

"An interesting theory," he observed. "I'm not sure that you can prove it, though."

"I think I can," Kendall said confidently.

He just "hmmed" at her. It was a low, sort of rumbly sound that emanated from his chest and ended in a vibration behind his lips.

Kendall, who had been congratulating herself on her admirable professional attitude thus far, felt herself slipping. It was only by sheer force of will that she managed to keep her body from shivering in reaction to the sound. She forced her eyes to stay fixed on his tie.

Chloe, who had remained silent throughout this exchange, now piped up. "She's not asking us to believe in her theories, Jared, just to agree to be trained in her evaluation method to see if there's a basis for proving accuracy. In fact, it might be better that you're skeptical."

Jared's gaze swung to Chloe. "Aren't you?"

"Maybe. A little. But then, I've already begun studying Kendall's research. It's fascinating. Besides, if you can do this for Kendall, Kendall can do something for you."

Now Kendall was looking at Chloe. "I can?"

"Sure. Jared just lost a subject for his experiments on dreaming."

Kendall's gray eyes grew huge in her small face. Chloe had lost her mind. "Chloe, I don't think that's a very good idea."

"Sure it is."

Jared sighed. "I didn't really want to use psychologists, or even psychology students, in my experiment. If they know too much about what I'm doing, that knowledge could influence their responses."

Just as Kendall was breathing a sigh of relief and trying to think up a reply that would sound sympathetic, Chloe butted in again. "Yes, but how many of your current dreamers are precognitive?"

A silence descended upon them as Kendall stared at her traitorous friend and Jared stared at Kendall.

"Really?"

"Chloe," Kendall muttered, "I think you and I should have a little talk."

Chloe just looked at her, and Kendall could tell that she was daring her to take up the challenge.

Jared continued to watch Kendall with growing curiosity. "Are you really precognitive?"

Shifting uncomfortably, Kendall shrugged. "Sometimes. But it isn't something I can control. Sometimes I don't remember the dream, just the feeling."

"And sometimes she's deadly accurate," Chloe offered. "She dreamed that we'd get a cat. She even described him. Three days later, there Boris sat on our porch. Then she dreamed that I was getting married. She even told me what his name was. I met my fiancé a week later. Call me crazy, but I fell like a lump of lead for Brice and would have even if I hadn't been forewarned."

"Anything else?" Jared asked.

Kendall felt like running and hiding. "Yes, but what difference does it make? I dream lots of things that never come true."

"How old are you?"

His abrupt question caused her to start slightly and her gray eyes narrowed in confusion. "My age? I'm twenty-five. Why?"

"That's pretty young for a Ph.D."

"I got through school early," she defended.

"So did I." He laughed. "Actually, the reason I asked was that I've broken my subjects down into general age groups so that no one age group takes precedence. And my eighteen-to-twenty-five-year-old female lot was just vacated a little while ago."

Chloe rose then and smiled. "I'm really sorry, but I have a class to teach in a few minutes."

Jared nodded and opened the door for her. "I didn't mean to keep you."

"Oh, that's all right. And I'll see you later, Kendall. Let me know what you two decide."

"You'll be the first to know, believe me," Kendall assured her.

After shutting the door behind Chloe, Jared returned to his desk and sat on it. "Wouldn't you be more comfortable sitting?"

"I doubt it," Kendall mumbled, but she sat, anyway.

"I have to say, I'm more than a little intrigued by all of this. But before we get into it, I should tell you about my project. And I assume that you're going to apply for the grant, as well?"

Kendall nodded. "Yes. So is Chloe."

"Okay. And that doesn't bother you?"

"No. It's not as if we would all be trying to ruin each other's projects."

"No, but someone has to win."

"And everyone else won't."

Jared smiled. "You're right about that. Okay. As for my project—since you're a psychologist, I assume that you've studied sleep and dreaming?"

Kendall nodded and tried not to look too interested, even though she was. "Yes. Dreams have been interpreted for ages, from biblical times to the revelations of Freud and Jung. But it was only about twenty-five years ago that science really discovered to what degrees we dream and the physiological and neurological changes we go through while in the dream state."

Leaning forward with his elbows resting on his knees, Jared's eyes positively sparkled as he spoke about his pet project. "Yes, exactly. We all know that everyone dreams. The extent of each person's memory of their dreams is varied, though. What I'm trying to do is discover to what degree the things we do during the day affect what we dream at night. And whether or not we can control our dreams. Are our dreams programmable? And if they are, how can we, as psychologists, develop that programmability to help patients overcome their problems?"

Kendall could understand why Jared spent so much time in his lab. His work was fascinating. And with research in his field still relatively recent, there was much to learn and discover.

"It's a fascinating subject," she agreed with a smile of envy. "How far have you gotten in your testing?"

He frowned suddenly. "Actually the subject testing only began last week. I've been laying the groundwork and doing research for the past year. Then I interviewed and hired subjects. And now I'm one short. And here you are, not only the right age, but with the added bonus of possible precognitive abilities. You're a dream come true."

Only a split second passed before Kendall burst out laughing. "Nobody warned me that you were a punster."

"At least you have a sense of humor. Most people don't get them."

"Maybe they have more sophisticated senses of humor."

"No, they're just no fun."

"And you are?"

"Definitely. Infinitely. But to get back to the point—I think I can live with the astrology thing if you can stand my recording your dreams."

Her light mood started to retreat. Jared couldn't know that she had already dreamed about him. "Uh, exactly how do you record them?"

"Nothing fancy." He smiled. "You wake up and relate your dreams and they're recorded. As much as I'd like to sometimes, I can't read minds—yet."

His eyes made a thorough and leisurely tour of her body from her toes to her shining hair, and Kendall knew that he was remembering her perusal of him the day before. Embarrassment burned her cheeks, but she fought it down. He couldn't embarrass her if she didn't let him. And she didn't really see how she could be a part of his experiment. She couldn't let him watch her while she slept. She couldn't describe her dreams to him. Especially if they were like the ones she'd already had about him!

As Kendall floundered around trying desperately to think of a way to get herself out of being *his* subject while at the same time have him agree to help *her,* Jared just waited. And watched. He looked perfectly content to watch her figuratively chase her tail, Kendall decided.

"Are you sure you wouldn't rather have someone outside the department?" she said at last.

He smiled at her half-hopeful suggestion. "No, not with the prospect of your possible precognitive abilities. Besides, as a psychologist, you might be able to offer some insights."

Not liking being in the position of having to trade favors for her project's survival, Kendall nevertheless realized that she was in desperate straits. It was small consolation that Jared was in the same position, because if she turned him down, he could find someone else in a few days, and Kendall didn't have that option.

So she tried to look at the situation positively. She would have a great test subject, and at the same time she might be able to learn more about sleep and dreaming. And maybe she wouldn't dream about him at all under controlled circumstances. And if she did... well, she'd cross that subconscious bridge when she came to it.

"All right," she said finally, and Jared nodded. He'd known she had no choice.

"Good," he said briskly. "And now, let's get down to business. Can you tell me what my astrological sign is?"

Kendall's throat suddenly went dry. A practical test of her theory. She was afraid of finding out it wouldn't work, but at the same time, she thought this was something she could do. Reaching for her book bag, Kendall opened it and pulled out a folder, from which she retrieved a sheet of paper. It was the form she'd given to 250 anonymous people. Now she handed it to Jared.

"I devised this survey to provide a very basic personality profile. There's a confidentiality statement at the top, and no names are given. Only some statistics and personality traits."

She handed him a pencil and he quirked his eyebrow at her in amusement. But then he turned and began swiftly ticking off answers to the multiple-choice questions. There were twenty of them, ranging in subject from a series of typical   what-would-you-take-with-you-to-a-deserted-island-for-a-year type, to a would-you-return-a-lost-wallet type.

When Jared handed her back the questionnaire, Kendall looked through all the answers he'd given. He'd chosen the Encyclopaedia Britannica for his deserted island and, of course, he would return the wallet. But Kendall had already known this. She'd been covertly observing him since September, and she'd already formed a secret opinion of his personality.

"Well?"

He didn't expect her to do it, she thought. If she was wrong, it could prove devastating to her research. But Kendall didn't think she was wrong.

"You're a Libra," she said quietly, but firmly. "It's the sign of balance, of fairness, which is why students rarely complain of the grades you give them. Libra is an air sign, and air translates into a freedom of movement, especially intellectually. Hence, you like working at the university, especially because of the independence that research offers. You're an excellent arbitrator, which is why you're such a good teacher.

"Libra is also a cardinal sign. That generally indicates a born leader, which you are. To be truly happy you have to be the boss or be self-employed. You, Dr. Dalton, have managed to be your own boss within your lab, and at the same time, you are most likely going to take over from Dr. Grady as the head of the psychology department when he retires. But that's not really news, since it's the generally accepted opinion of the faculty, anyway."

She could have told him more, but chose not to. She watched his expression. She had to be right, she told herself. All the indications were there. She forced herself not to ask him if she was. Instead she pulled a small envelope from her folder.

"There's a card in this envelope with a number on it that corresponds with a number on the form you filled out. If I had given you this for my survey, I would have asked you to write your birthdate on the card and seal it in the envelope and then return them together. When the surveys are evaluated, we'll determine which sign a person is and write it on the form. When we're finished with all the questionnaires, I'll open the envelopes and calculate the accuracy. Then I'll determine how well my theory works."

"I still don't know if I have much confidence in the field, but you've surprised me, Kendall. Though you were probably guessing, you *are* right. I was born October fifteenth, and that makes me a Libra."

Kendall just smiled. She felt more than relief, she thought as he smiled back. It was almost elation. It was the thrill that her research wasn't off track and that she was accomplishing something tangible. She'd passed the test she'd created for herself, and she'd done it with a formidable audience. If it hadn't been against her personal rule, she would have kissed Jared Dalton.

"And what is your sign and what does that mean?" he asked.

She opened her mouth to tell him, and then closed it. "That's what you're going to be doing as part of my project. After studying the material I've prepared and applying it to the personality-trait form, you should be able to tell me."

Jared laughed. "I think, Kendall, that the next few months are going to prove very interesting—for both of us. I might be skeptical, but I will be open-minded about your project. And I expect the same from you."

Kendall had no doubt their time together would be interesting, and she'd do what she could to help him, too. She just hoped that she could keep her attraction for Jared a secret through it all. She wondered if it would make a difference. He wasn't interested in her; he hadn't even remembered her name. But he had remembered where they'd met, she reminded herself. And at least she didn't bore him, she thought with satisfaction. Maybe they could even be friends of a sort.

"I'll need you to sleep here in the lab three nights a week. I hope that won't cause too much disruption in your personal life."

Kendall thought about Chloe and Boris and decided that there was a minimum of disruption on that front. The main disruption would be within herself.

"No, it won't. Although I have to tell you that I only remember my dreams once in a while and that they're sometimes disjointed and don't make a bit of sense to me."

"I think you'll find that might change during these experiments. If my theory is right, and I think it is, we can all control our own dreams if we decide we want to and instruct our minds to follow our wishes."

Kendall hoped he was right. If so, she could instruct her wayward mind to stop thinking about him all the time. "It sounds very interesting. When did you want me to start?"

"Tonight, if you can. I need to get you into the program as soon as possible, since the other subjects have already been through two sessions each."

"Do I just show up here with my jammies and toothbrush?"

She was trying not to be nervous and almost managed it, but Jared wasn't a psychologist for nothing. "Don't worry. It's not as intimidating as it sounds. My lab has been outfitted specifically for this project. There are simulated bedrooms with different decors and bathrooms. Wear what you usually wear to sleep in, and bring your own pillow if you like.''

Kendall was still having problems with the idea, but she was certain that she was mature enough to handle it. She would just put aside her personal feelings and treat this like a job that had to be done.

''What time should I be here?''

''What time do you normally go to bed?''

She swallowed nervously and shrugged. ''I guess around eleven or midnight. It depends on how much work I have to do, or if I've gone out somewhere.''

''Then come around ten-thirty or eleven. Do you want me to pick you up?''

''No, I only live a few blocks away. I can walk.''

Jared was frowning. ''I don't know that I like the idea of your walking even a few blocks by yourself at night. I'll pick you up.''

''That's all right, really. I can walk.''

''Then I'll walk with you.''

Knowing he wasn't going to back down, Kendall sighed and recited her address. ''I live in a small bungalow with Chloe,'' she added. ''Come by any time after ten.''

With that she rose and picked up her bag, draping its straps over her shoulder. ''Thank you for agreeing to be a part of my project. I guess you know how much this means to me.''

''Yes, I think I do. Don't forget—we both win in this.''

''Right. I'll see you tonight.''

With that, she left his office and headed back up the stairs. She had a feeling she was going to regret this before all was said and done. However, since she couldn't come up with another way to complete her project and since she wanted to apply for the grant, she had no choice.

She stopped back by the office to pick up one of the grant applications before going upstairs to the faculty lounge. As she headed up the stairs, she wondered how she was going to cope with the coming project. She hated being backed into a corner, but at the same time, the thought of seeing Jared Dalton almost every day was exciting. She might have had rules about not dating a coworker, but she had no rules about looking.

Kendall was about to leave the lounge fifteen minutes later for the lab when Chloe appeared.

"Well, if it isn't Benedict Chloe."

"Aw, come on, Kendall, you aren't really angry, are you? I mean, I did it for your own good. And you have to admit that it seemed perfect. You need him and he needs you."

"All right, all right," Kendall conceded. "So it seemed perfect, and we did agree to help each other out. But I should still be mad at you for taking over like that."

"I had to," Chloe insisted. "You looked like your knees were about to buckle at any minute."

Kendall was horrified. "I didn't."

"Well, maybe not to somebody who didn't know you. But I knew you were freaking out on the inside."

"I'm *still* freaking out." Kendall sighed. "And I think it's going to get worse before it gets any better. Especially since I have to start dreaming for him tonight."

"Tonight? He doesn't waste any time, does he?"

"Well, since he started this phase of his experiment last week, he couldn't really afford to, could he?"

Chloe looked uncertain for a moment. "You aren't really mad at me, are you?"

"I should be. But since you probably saved my project and made it possible for it not only to be completed, but for me to apply for the grant, too... Well, it seems that I would appear a bit ungrateful if I were to be angry with you.''

Laughing, Chloe hugged her. ''Oh, I'm so glad.''

''Just don't try it again.''

Chapter Three

Jared fiddled with some dials on a monitoring machine and wondered if he'd regret making this deal with Kendall Arden. He'd promised to help her, though, and he would. But this was still astrology and he couldn't help but be skeptical about it.

Skeptical, but intrigued. If nothing else, her research should be interesting reading. As interesting as the woman herself.

"Are you sure you aren't going to need me tonight, Jared?"

Jared looked up at his graduate-student assistant in the project and shook his head. "I can handle it, Larry. There's only one subject tonight."

"Right. The last-minute substitution for subject number six."

Regarding his assistant with a wry grin, Jared said, "You know, Larry, I think you've been hanging around this lab and your statistics classes too long. Subject six had a name."

Larry frowned. "I suppose she did. What was it?"

Staring at Larry's expectant features, Jared shrugged. "I have no idea. I'd have to look it up."

Pulling his coat off the rack next to the office door, Larry grinned. "Never mind. Onward and upward. How'd you find a substitute so quickly?"

"You might say that she was found for me." Jared smiled.

"Who knew you needed a replacement part for the project?"

Jared scowled at Larry's choice of words. He made it sound as if the people participating in the project were just numbers, not individuals. Jared hoped that wasn't true. He would have to look into it and make an effort to be more aware and sensitive. Psychology was, after all, the study of human behavior.

"Dr. Munson suggested that Dr. Arden and I help each other out. She needed a subject for her project, too."

Larry seemed confused. "Kendall? But she's researching something about astrology, isn't she?"

Frowning at Larry, Jared said, "Yes, she is. And I didn't realize you knew her so well."

"Oh, because I call her Kendall instead of Dr.? She says she'd rather be called by her first name, especially since most of the grad students are only a year or so younger than she is. Sharon's older than her. Besides, Kendall's a lot of fun. She's a great kidder."

"I take it you're not in any of her classes?"

Larry looked offended. "Of course not. She teaches freshman and sophomores."

Jared grinned. "Oh, right. I beg your pardon."

"Anyway, I knew she was researching astrology and that none of the faculty, apart from Chloe Munson, would give her the time of day. So why are you?"

"Maybe I'm trying to remind myself that as a scientist and psychologist I should be more open-minded."

Larry didn't look convinced. Tossing his coat back on the rack, he pulled a straight chair from its place against the wall and turned it around, straddling it to face Jared. "Pardon me if I'm being presumptuous, Dr. Dalton, but are you sure you aren't being swayed by a pair of big blue eyes?"

"They're gray."

"What?"

Jared, realizing what he'd just said, shrugged. "Nothing. And I haven't been swayed by Kendall Arden. At least not by her looks. She's precognitive."

Larry stared for a moment, then grinned. "You're kidding, right?"

"Not unless she is, and I don't think she is. Besides, Chloe Munson has confirmed that Kendall had at least two precognitive dreams last fall that were right on the money. I haven't had a chance to ask if she's had any since then."

"That's amazing," Larry exclaimed. "I had no idea. This is great. The possibilities for this project are now fantastic."

Jared nodded, unable to contain his enthusiasm. "I know. Trying to control what we dream is exciting in and of itself. But the possibility of being able to control precognition is beyond anything I'd hoped for."

"No wonder you agreed to be subjected to astrology," Larry murmured. "But I do have a question about that. Isn't it like a conflict of interest or something, since you're both competing for that grant Gundersson left the university?"

Knowing he shouldn't be surprised by how quickly the students learned of faculty news, Jared was nonetheless impressed. "Are you sure you didn't know about the grant before the meeting?"

"Naw. It took us until about fifteen minutes after the meeting was over. So, is that okay? I mean the fact that both of you are in each other's projects and also competing for the grant? That's a lot of money."

"I know. But I don't think there's a conflict of interest. Not since we're both on the same ground."

"But what if she, you know, sabotages your project?"

Jared hadn't considered that. It hadn't occurred to him that Kendall would do something like that. "Since I have the power to ruin hers, too, I doubt that would happen. Do you think Kendall is capable of that?"

Larry shook his head. "No. She's got too much Pollyanna in her. But I thought you should consider all angles."

"Thanks, Larry," Jared said dryly.

"No problem. I'll see you tomorrow."

With that, Larry was gone, and Jared spent a few minutes wondering why it was that he seemed to be the only one who didn't know Kendall Arden. True, she'd been at CSU for just six months and he had been busy during that time with his project research, but Larry and Chloe and Millie and, no doubt, several others had managed to get to know her quite well.

Feeling as though he had missed out on something very important, Jared decided to come out of his lab a little more often and mingle with the faculty and staff, as well as the students. Just as soon as this project was completed, he'd try to be more social.

Of course, then it would be summer and school would be out and he would be sailing and doing other research.

He wondered what Kendall was planning to do during the summer. Maybe she was going out with someone. Was she dating some man regularly? Were they lovers?

Probably, he thought crossly. Kendall Arden was a very attractive woman. And he was attracted to her. Then he grinned. She was attracted to him, as well. Jared smiled as he remembered how she'd been looking at him the day before when she'd thought he wasn't aware. His smile got even wider as he recalled her acute embarrassment at being caught.

Now that he thought about it, Kendall's precognitive abilities weren't the only avenues with possibilities.

"I know that I'm the one who got you into all of this, but given how nervous you seem around him, are you going to be able to sleep while he's watching you?"

Kendall sighed as she tossed her sleeveless cotton nightdress into a backpack. "I don't know, Chloe. I'm hoping that enforced proximity will make him seem boring to me."

Her roommate didn't look convinced. "Right. And do you actually have any confidence whatsoever that this theory will prove true?"

"No, I don't." Her toothbrush and toothpaste joined the nightdress. "But since I can't come up with a viable alternative, I'm just going to have to deal with it and hope I don't make a fool of myself in the process."

Boris jumped onto the bed and pushed his head into Chloe's hand. She stroked him absently as she watched Kendall put a few other items into her backpack before zipping it.

"You've said a lot about keeping your feelings hidden, but what if he comes on to you?"

Kendall paused and turned to stare at Chloe. "He won't."

"But what if he does?"

As much as it pained her to admit it, she said, "He won't because he isn't attracted to me, Chloe. I mean, come on, I've been here for six months and he couldn't even remember my name. And not that it makes any difference, but even if he were interested in me and asked me out, I'd still say no."

"You can't judge every man by the conduct of one who was a jerk in your past."

"I know that," Kendall answered calmly. "But after having to deal with the stress that kind of situation puts on my work, I believe that keeping my romantic life and my professional life distinctly separate is the right thing for me."

"Sure. But since he's a Libra and all, don't you think that he'd be too innately fair to pull something like that other guy did?"

Pausing, Kendall nodded. "True. However, just because I don't believe he'd do anything deliberately doesn't mean it still couldn't happen. When human egos start getting bumped around, even the most fair-minded man can become unpredictable."

"Well, that's true. I just hope you won't be hurt by any of this, Kendall."

"I hope I won't, either. And I still think that we're both talking about something that isn't going to happen, because Jared Dalton isn't interested in me as anything more than a guinea pig."

Hearing the knock on the front door, Kendall looked at the clock on her nightstand. Ten-thirty. Chloe rose and headed for the living room when the phone rang.

"I'll get it," she said. "It's probably Brice. He's coming over for dinner later."

"Is he bringing the TV dinners?" Kendall joked.

"Very funny," Chloe said as she picked up the receiver.

Pulling open the door, Kendall noticed that the doorway seemed to have shrunk. Jared wasn't an enormous man—around six feet and one hundred eighty pounds—but he seemed to overwhelm the space before her. He looked extremely fit, she thought. If he didn't swim, he was probably a runner.

Stepping back hastily to allow him entrance, Kendall gestured toward her serenely smiling roommate, who was on the telephone. "Come on in. Have a seat, and I'll just get my things and be right back."

Boris chose that moment to jump down from the sofa and take a swipe at Jared's pants leg. Jared looked down and laughed. "Hey, you. These pants are not cheap."

He bent down and picked up the heavy gray cat. Kendall held her breath, waiting for Boris to scratch or bite him. But he did neither. He merely yawned greatly and began some substantial purring.

"I guess he likes me."

Chloe had just hung up the phone, and she and Kendall glanced at each other and laughed. "You and nobody else," said Kendall.

"Yes, Boris isn't known for his acceptance of people in general," Chloe added. "Do you have pets, Jared?"

"Not really. I have Harpo, but he's not a normal sort of pet."

"What do you mean?"

Jared grinned. "I mean he's a bird. A cockatoo, to be exact. My cousin gave him to me two months ago for Christmas."

"How interesting!" Chloe exclaimed. "Does he talk?"

"No," Jared replied. "He whistles, but no amount of coaxing or cajoling has brought forth speech. I think he's a dud."

"He probably senses that you have no confidence in him and feels unloved," Chloe suggested.

Jared blinked at her. "Really? You haven't studied psychology by any chance, have you?"

They all laughed and Chloe reached over and pulled her sketchbook from Boris's teeth. "I had to study something when I discovered I wasn't good enough to be an artist."

Taking the sketches from her, Jared scrutinized the one Chloe had been working on. "Isn't that a subjective thing? I mean, how good an artist is?"

Chloe smiled. "Yes. But I wasn't as good as I thought I should be."

"So now she does art therapy with kids," Kendall explained.

"Oh, right, your specialty being child psychology."

"I'll be right back," Kendall said and slipped away to retrieve her backpack. A few seconds later, she returned and found Chloe showing Jared a drawing she'd done of Kendall. It was a lazy sort of sketch, with Kendall lying on the grass in the backyard, a blade of grass between her teeth.

"This is wonderful," Jared was saying.

"That's what I think," Chloe returned. "But Kendall won't let me hang it."

Embarrassed, Kendall refused to look at the sketch. "I don't think it looks like me."

Jared looked at the sensuality Chloe had captured in the drawing, then back at Kendall. "Oh, I don't know. I think it does. We don't all look the same all the time, you know."

Kendall didn't comment. She just picked up her pack and slung it over her shoulder. Chloe stood by the door as they left. "Now you sleep well tonight."

"Ha-ha," Kendall said, and shut the door behind her.

Standing on the porch next to her, Jared laughed softly. "You seem to be very good friends."

"We are. It was a godsend to me that Chloe needed a roommate at a time when I was new in town and at the university. She's made everything easier for me."

Stepping off the porch, Jared led the way to the sidewalk, where they fell into step beside each other. Kendall was doing her best to keep her hand from accidentally brushing his as they walked, but she wasn't being very successful. And with every brush of his skin against hers, Kendall's heart skipped a beat. She shuddered to think what would happen if he kissed her. She'd probably die of a coronary on the spot.

"I hope you're not too apprehensive about tonight."

The sound of his voice cutting through the silence startled her, but she hoped he hadn't noticed. "I, uh, well, maybe I am. A little."

"Don't worry. It's to be expected. And it's part of my project's findings, as well."

By now they had reached the psychology building and Jared led her around to a side door. He pulled out a key and opened the door, then led her down a dimly lit stone stairway. Why was she suddenly wondering if Jared's lab was rather Frankensteinesque? Kendall shivered as she felt the cinder-block walls seem to close in on her.

"Sorry about taking you in this way," Jared was saying, "but it's quicker. The decor is sadly lacking. I couldn't manage to figure out a way to get the university to pay for the interior decoration of a stairway and corridors."

At the bottom of the stairs they walked briefly along a short corridor to a knobless door that Jared unlocked and pushed open. Kendall's eyes scanned the area curiously. Dr. Dalton's laboratory.

It wasn't exactly what she expected. There was a massive desk with an expensive powerful computer on it, and several machines with blinking lights. Against one wall were three television monitors, which were now blank. A bookcase behind the desk held dozens of technical manuals and textbooks. A filing cabinet sat in one corner with a potted plant atop it. Kendall wondered if it was fake, since there were no windows.

One wall had three doors in it, all of them closed. Another wall had one door. It probably led to his office, she surmised.

All in all, it didn't look like a laboratory, Kendall thought. It looked like someone's living room. A very high-tech living room, but hardly the sterile conditions most scientists worked in.

"Where's Igor?"

Jared blinked at her, then smiled. "Oh, you mean Larry. He went home. I told him I could handle you alone. I can, can't I? You're not going to get too rowdy tonight, are you?"

Kendall was in the middle of gasping with indignation when she realized he was teasing her. Schooling her features into a prim facade, she said, "I don't know. Maybe. Aren't there any other subjects here?"

"No, not tonight. One of them had to reschedule for personal reasons. That's why I sent Larry home. Usually both of us stay here all night, monitoring subjects. Then we sleep until late afternoon and come back to evaluate our findings early the next evening."

"It must be difficult to try to readjust your own sleeping patterns like that," she offered, unable to think of anything else to stave off the dreaded silence.

"After a week or so, it wasn't hard. Now, why don't I show you where you'll be sleeping?"

Or where I'll be trying to sleep, Kendall thought.

Jared walked toward the wall with the three doors, and Kendall suddenly wondered if he would choose door number one, door number two, or—for the big prize—door number three.

He chose door number three.

Kendall watched as Jared opened the door and turned on a light from a wall switch. He then gestured for her to enter. Kendall smiled and hoped she looked more confident than she felt.

The room was like any bedroom in any woman's home. A woman's home because it was color-coordinated and homey. There were curtains that matched the wildflower print of the ruffled skirt and comforter on the bed. A white wicker nightstand was positioned beside the bed, and the base of the lamp on it had a soft, wildflower design. To top it all off, a vase of real flowers had been carefully placed on the nightstand, as well.

The sheets, which had been turned down, were crisp and white. There were several pillows of various sizes that lay against the wicker headboard of the bed. On the other side of the bed, next to the window, was a huge plant, more like a tree really. The curtains were closed, and Kendall knew that there wasn't really a window behind the curtains, but it looked nice, anyway.

"This is lovely," she said softly. "Who's your decorator?"

Jared laughed. "A department-store catalogue. We just ordered everything and they delivered it. The bathroom is through that door."

Following his gesture, Kendall walked over and pushed open the door, which was standing ajar. She turned on the light and saw that the decor was continued in the bathroom with its white wicker furnishings and the wildflower shower curtain. Fluffy white towels hung next to the basin, and Kendall was sure that there would be bath salts and perfumed soap waiting, too.

She turned back and smiled wryly at Jared. "This is better than home."

He was relieved she approved, she thought, but he only nodded.

"We've tried to make the room as comfortable as possible so that the subjects can relax enough to fall asleep easily."

Kendall looked around the room, but didn't let her gaze linger on the ventilation grates or the large mirror that hung over the white dresser on the wall opposite the bed. She knew that video cameras were trained on the bed to record the sleeping subjects, but she didn't want to acknowledge their presence. It was bad enough that she was aware of their existence.

Dropping her backpack onto the bed, Kendall sat on the edge and looked at Jared expectantly. He sat in the only chair in the room, a wicker armchair with wildflower-covered cushions, and leaned forward.

"I know you understand the basics of sleep and dreaming." When Kendall nodded, he went on. "We already understand that everybody goes through four stages of sleep, from light sleep to deep sleep, and that there are two states of sleep, dreaming and nondreaming. The dream stage is called REM—rapid eye movement—which I'm sure you've heard of. Dream researchers have already proven all of that through the use of electroencephalographs, or EEGs. We also know that everybody dreams four or five times a night or more, even though those dreams might not be remembered.

"What this project is concerned with is whether or not we can learn to control what we dream. And, in so doing, can we help people to work through psychologic disorders by using that control?"

Kendall was raptly attentive. She wanted to know more about his methods and conclusions. "How are you monitoring the dreams? And how are you interpreting them? Are you using subliminal sounds after sleep begins? Or other physical—"

"Hey, whoa, you're the subject in this experiment, not the psychologist," Jared teased, amusement in his eyes at her enthusiasm.

Kendall grinned sheepishly. "Sorry. I tend to get carried away when I get close to something this fascinating."

"That's all right. But if you're so interested, why do you seem so apprehensive?"

Kendall worried the inside of her lip with her teeth. "I am nervous," she admitted. "But this afternoon I wasn't as clear on your methods in this experiment. I was wary of a stark mattress and EEG wires taped all over my head."

Jared laughed. "No, none of that. Basically, I'm studying cause and effect and beyond that, if we can control that cause and effect."

"And so far?"

"So far we've barely gotten started. All the subjects have had only two or three sleep sessions each, so we're just getting under way."

He rose and walked over to the nightstand, where he opened a drawer and pulled out a clipboard. A pen and a

white sheet of paper were attached to it. He extended it
toward Kendall. She took the clipboard and examined the
form that was on it.

"You want to know what I ate for dinner?"

"Of course," Jared said. "What you eat can definitely
affect what you dream and how much you remember.
There are also questions on there about your state of mind
on the day of each test. How would you describe your state
of mind today, Kendall?"

Looking from the form to Jared and back, Kendall
shook her head. She picked up the pen and wrote: *Uncertainty and a sense of losing control over my project. Tense.*

She failed to mention the erratic beating of her heart and
the warmth she felt whenever she was near Jared. He'd
have to resort to studying parapsychology and mind reading to get that out of her, she decided.

Jotting down the ingredients of the fast-food dinner
she'd had that evening, she handed the clipboard back to
Jared and watched him read it. If she expected a reaction,
she was disappointed. He merely tore the top sheet off and
replaced the clipboard in the nightstand drawer.

"That's it for tonight," he said as he headed for the
door. "Since this is your first night as a subject, I'll mainly
just monitor your sleep patterns and timetable. How long
it takes you to fall asleep, how long your REM stages last,
and how many times you dream in a night. If you happen
to wake up after a dream, just review it in your head, and
then describe it out loud in as much detail as possible.
Voice-activated tape recorders will make sure we get it all.
Okay?"

Kendall nodded. "Sure. What time will I be woken?"

Jared looked at his watch. "It's almost eleven-thirty.
How about eight?"

"All right. But I may wake up before that."

"That's fine." His eyes narrowed on her face, and Kendall wondered if he could sense her apprehension. "Good night, Kendall."

"Good night."

Then he was gone, shutting the door behind him. Kendall tried to ignore the fact that she was going to be watched all night as the sensitive video cameras recorded her REMs so that Jared would know when she was dreaming.

Shuddering slightly, she turned and snagged her backpack and carried it into the bathroom.

While brushing her teeth and washing her face, she tried to relax. The whole session would be a disaster if she lay awake all night.

Pulling off her clothes, she slipped into her nightgown and hoped it wasn't too sheer. She'd chosen the most demure of her nightgowns, not wanting Jared to think she was trying to appear sexy, but at the same time, not wanting to appear as though she was trying *not* to appear sexy.

Frowning at her convoluted thoughts, she shut off the light and made her way into the bedroom, clutching a batch of tests she needed to grade and her gradebook, which she'd pulled from her backpack. No reason not to get some work done while she was trying to convince herself that she was sleepy.

After only twenty minutes of trying to concentrate on correcting papers, Kendall realized that the mental stress of the day had taken a real toll on her body and that she was, indeed, tired.

She closed her gradebook and placed it along with the tests on the nightstand. She then slid her legs between the covers and tossed most of the pillows onto the floor. She reached over and switched off the lamp, pausing to inhale the scent of the wildflowers as she did so.

The whole setup had to have been masterminded by a Libra, she thought idly as she snuggled down. The decor of this room, and especially the flowers, were the mark of a person who appreciated beauty and the comfort of beautiful things.

Did Jared think *she* was beautiful, Kendall wondered as she drifted into sleep....

She was beautiful, Jared thought as he watched the monitor on his right. The infrared light wasn't the most flattering to human skin, but Kendall was lovely in spite of it.

Scowling at his unprofessional thoughts, Jared adjusted one camera for a close-up of Kendall's face, and the other to include a shot of her entire body. Body position and movement in sleep could also affect dreaming.

She was just now entering the first stage of sleep and it would most likely be an hour before she entered stage four of sleep and began dreaming.

He adjusted a few dials and absently watched Kendall. She was lying on her back, one arm beside her head on the pillow, the other resting on her rib cage. There was a slight frown on her face.

Jared hadn't expected Kendall to be so interested in his project. It made him feel a bit guilty for the complete lack of enthusiasm he felt over the prospect of his having to learn more than he wanted to know about astrological traits.

But here they both were and there was no backing out now for either of them. They were both professionals and there was no reason the next few months shouldn't be a positive experience.

The fact that he was attracted to her was neither here nor there, although it probably would have been better if he wasn't. It was also probably a good idea not to pursue that attraction. Kendall seemed quite intent upon ignoring her attraction for him. Jared wasn't sure he liked that. Even if her decision was for the best, he didn't like ignoring his feelings, or being ignored, either.

Kendall moaned and turned over in her sleep, pulling her pillow close to her chest. Jared's eyes were on the monitor and he swallowed. She was sexy enough in her everyday skirt and sweater, but dressed in a sleeveless cotton nightgown that gaped open over her upper chest, Jared thought he'd never seen a sexier woman. Why hadn't he noticed her before?

"Get a grip," he whispered to himself.

Forcing his mind to concentrate on her closed eyes, he refused to let his thoughts wander again. There was work to be done, data to be gathered, and tests to be run.

Speculations about the sexiness of Kendall Arden were regretfully dismissed.

Chapter Four

*K*endall was walking down a corridor, at the end of which was an open door. Inside were members of the award committee for the grant. They were screening the applicants.

They were all sitting in the room and waiting for her. Kendall was walking toward the room, but with every step she took, the room seemed farther away.

She was carrying the results of her project. She looked down at them and was horrified to notice that the cover page was blank. Flipping through the pages she saw that whole sections were blank.

Suddenly at her feet were piles of books and papers. Research notes swirled around her, just out of reach. As she lunged for the bits of paper, several others swirled up from the floor. She could see disjointed phrases and knew that the papers were supposed to be included in her findings.

Inside the room, the committee members looked irritated. They glanced at their watches and shrugged. They were talking, but Kendall couldn't hear them because the papers around her were causing whirlpools of air currents, which roared past her ears.

Finally she was able to grasp one of the pieces of paper as it darted before her eyes. She looked hopefully down the corridor, but the committee members were filing out of the room. They were leaving! She hadn't turned her project in by the deadline! Trying to call out to them, she discovered her voice didn't work. Gathering all her strength, she tried to run toward them, but tripped over a stack of books and began to fall. . . .

With a jerk and a small gasp, Kendall awoke and tried to figure out where she was. Her heart was beating so hard that the blood roared in her ears. It was only a dream, she told herself. She still had plenty of time to complete and turn in her project. They were all due May first, with the grant to be awarded June first. It was still only mid-February.

Opening her eyes, she suddenly remembered where she was. The experiment. What had Jared said? To remember the details of a dream and then just to recite it. She felt stupid, but she closed her eyes and cleared her throat.

"I don't know if you're listening, but I just woke up from a dream. Although, to me, I suppose it might be better termed a nightmare."

She then related the dream, including as many details as she could recall, including her feelings as well as what was happening and who was in it.

When she finished, she waited, unsure about what she was supposed to do next. Should she wait to see if Jared was going to say or do something? It was dark. What time was it? She reached for her watch on the nightstand and read its illuminated dial. Seven-thirty.

Sitting up and reaching over, she snapped on the lamp and let her eyes adjust to the muted light. He still hadn't said anything. Should she just get up and take a shower and go into the next room?

As she sat there debating her next move, she heard a soft clicking sound and then Jared's disembodied voice floated into the room. "Good morning, Kendall. You did great. I was just making a few notes. If you'd like breakfast, I'm going out to get some."

Kendall didn't know where to look, and she felt uncomfortable talking to Jared without being able to see his face. Especially when he could see her.

Then the truth hit her. He could see her! Kendall barely stifled a groan of dismay. She knew what she looked like first thing in the morning, and it wasn't her best. Her hair would be mussed and probably sticking up at weird angles. Her eyes were most likely puffy and she wouldn't doubt it if there were creases on her cheek from sleeping on a fold in the sheet.

"Kendall? Do you want something to eat?"

"What? Uh, sure, I guess. Just hot chocolate and a cheese Danish, though. And maybe orange juice. Or a banana. Oh, whatever. You bring it and I'll probably eat it."

She thought she heard chuckling, then he said, "Okay. I'll be back in about thirty minutes."

If she expected to hear doors closing to signal his exit, she was disappointed. Yawning, she told herself that the bedrooms were, no doubt, soundproof.

Thirty minutes.

Thirty minutes? Kendall leapt out of bed and ran for the bathroom. It usually took her two hours to get ready in the morning. Of course, she defended herself as she turned on the taps in the shower, that was when she cooked her own breakfast and read the newspaper and watched the morning news shows.

After her shower, rummaging through the vanity in the bathroom proved fruitful, since she found a hair dryer, which she hadn't thought to pack. There were only so many things one could cram into a backpack.

After drying her hair and brushing her teeth, Kendall put on the fresh underwear she'd brought, and then stepped into the clothes she'd worn the day before. She'd just go home and change once she got there.

A little blush and lip gloss was all the makeup she had with her, so they would have to do. Luckily for Kendall, her eyelashes and eyebrows were naturally dark auburn in contrast with her strawberry-blond hair.

A rap on the door to the bedroom sent her scurrying out of the bathroom. She opened the bedroom door and Jared smiled down at her. Her heart tripped over itself and she found herself inhaling deeply. It didn't seem to matter that it was the end of a long workday for him. He looked wonderful.

"Look good?" he said.

"Wonderful," she sighed, then blinked up at him, her cheeks flushing. How... Then she saw he was looking at the food he'd laid out on the desk in the adjoining room. "Yes," Kendall said quickly. "And it smells good, too."

Jared walked back into the room and sat down behind the desk. Another chair had been placed at the end of the desk, and Kendall sank into it.

"I didn't rush you, did I?"

She smiled at his words. "Actually you did, but it's okay."

"Are you one of those poky people in the mornings?"

Reaching for a container of orange juice, Kendall scowled at him. "Yes, I am. I like to enjoy my breakfast and my paper. Sometimes I watch the morning shows for the weather or national news. And I like to take my time getting ready to go to class."

"Would you like me to bring a newspaper next time?"

Kendall had the feeling he was serious. "No, that's all right. I didn't say I needed to hang around here and do all of that. In fact, you really don't even have to bring me breakfast, although this is really nice."

"It's no trouble," Jared insisted.

"I know, but since I only live a few blocks away, it isn't any hardship to go home and eat."

"Whatever you're more comfortable with," he said, and tucked in to his breakfast.

Whatever she was comfortable with? "Comfortable" wasn't a word that sprang to mind when considering anything to do with Jared Dalton. Exciting, yes. Unpredictable, yes. Sensorial, yes. But comfortable?

Well, she thought as she bit into her cheese Danish, she wasn't uncomfortable sitting here eating breakfast with him.

She'd only been uncomfortable with one thing this morning. Now Kendall surprised herself by telling him about it. "Actually the only thing that bothered me with all this was knowing you could see me but I couldn't see you. And then hearing your voice, but not knowing where to look when I talked to you."

Jared nodded and swallowed a sip of coffee. "I know. But unless you want me to come into the bedroom and talk to you when you're still half-asleep, it's the only method we have of communicating."

Kendall was about to suggest that it could hardly make much difference whether he saw her on a monitor or in the flesh when she realized that the difference was phenomenal. No, she was better off talking to a disembodied voice.

"I guess you're right" was all she said.

"I wanted to tell you again that the way you described the dream you woke from was good. Too often people only remember the essence of a dream and the details are too quickly forgotten."

Kendall grimaced as she remembered the dream. "I wish that one was easily forgotten. It was the most depressing dream I've had in a long time."

"It's not surprising, though," Jared said. "With all that happened yesterday, and all the worrying you've been doing over your project, anyway, it isn't too surprising that those feelings of anxiousness should manifest themselves in a dream."

Nodding agreement, Kendall said, "Yes, I guess you're right. But if it's all the same to you, I'd rather not have a repeat of that particular dream."

"Well, that's up to you," he said. "If my theory proves true, we should be able to train ourselves to dream what we want."

Curious about how much he'd tested his theory, Kendall regarded him intently. "Can you do that? I mean, have you been able to control your own dreams?"

Jared shook his head. "Not really. By meditating and using relaxation exercises before I sleep, I have been able to dream what I tell myself to dream, but I haven't been able to control other dreams I have. And I'm not always able to wake up after every dream to record them. Although I keep a dream journal of those I do remember. That's why doing the experiments in these controlled circumstances is so important."

Kendall sighed. So much to think about. "I suppose that eventually you'll be waking me up four or five times a night and asking me to try to remember whatever dream I just had."

"Right. But that's in the last stages of the project. And hopefully, you'll be able to fall back to sleep quickly. Last night, for instance, you had five dream stages. Only the last one woke you up."

Hiding her curiosity wasn't something that Kendall was good at, even when it caused her embarrassment. Which was why she had to ask him about his viewing of her.

"Did you watch me all last night...just sleeping? I didn't do anything weird in my sleep, did I?"

Jared smiled—indulgently, Kendall thought. He'd probably been asked this question dozens of times. "Yes, I watched you. You weren't just sleeping, you were dreaming, too. And what do you mean, weird?"

"I don't know. I didn't drool or anything, did I?" She shuddered at the thought.

"Not that I noticed," he said with a straight face.

"Did I snore?"

"Well..."

"Oh, how embarrassing."

"No, no. Actually it wasn't snoring. More like heavy breathing."

Kendall wasn't sure how to take that. It made her sound like a pervert. "How heavy is heavy? I didn't sound like an obscene phone caller, did I?"

Jared just laughed and shook his head. "No, you didn't. The only thing I noticed that was at all unusual was that you moved around a lot."

Knowing that was true, Kendall nodded. "That happens all the time. My covers are always a mess."

Their breakfast finished, Kendall looked at her watch. Her eyes widened in alarm. "Tell me it's not really five 'till nine."

Jared looked at his own watch. "Sorry, I can't do that. It is five 'till. Now it's four 'till."

On her feet, Kendall ran back into the bedroom to retrieve her backpack. "I have a class upstairs at nine," she explained as she came back into the room.

"Oh. Sorry. I didn't realize I was keeping you."

Kendall blinked up at him. "Neither did I." She shook her head to clear it. It had a tendency to get muddled around Jared. "But I really do have to go. Thanks for breakfast, it was great. Sorry I couldn't make my bed. How do I get out of here?"

"You're welcome, we have maid service, and this way."

He held open the single door at the opposite wall and Kendall saw that it led into his office. From there, she knew the way up to the rest of the psych building.

"Thanks," she said, turning to leave. "Oh, when would I be back?"

"Tomorrow night," he said. "I'll pick you up at the same time, all right?"

"You really don't have to."

"You're late."

Kendall sighed and turned, running through a short hall and up the stairs. As she turned the corner to take the next flight up, she wondered if anyone would notice she was still wearing the clothes she'd worn the day before.

Chloe listened to Kendall's description of what had happened to her the previous night as she did a line sketch of Boris, who was draped over the ottoman, half-asleep, occasionally batting at some fringe that hung from the draperies behind him.

"I'm glad you didn't have any trouble falling asleep in those circumstances," Chloe murmured. "Although it sounds as if Jared has thought of everything, what with the room being so beautiful and comfortable."

"Oh, it was almost luxurious," Kendall assured her. "And I thought it would take me forever to fall asleep, too. But I guess I'd just been through too much during the day yesterday. I was mentally exhausted."

"That's true. Still, the thought of someone watching you while you sleep... It seems too much like Big Brother to me."

Kendall nodded. "That's what I thought at first. But I don't feel as though Jared is spying on me, really. He's observing my sleep patterns and my dream patterns. That's all."

"He didn't come on to you or say anything suggestive?"

"No, he didn't."

Chloe laughed. "You sound disappointed."

"I'm not," Kendall insisted. "Really. In fact, I think everything is going very smoothly. Tomorrow night, when I go back, I'm going to take some of my research notes for him to look over. He's going to have to become familiar with them if he's going to begin the training process for my project soon."

Boris yawned and reared his head briefly, then took another swipe at the curtains before turning over and jumping down from the ottoman. Chloe paused in her drawing, since her subject was gone, and looked directly at Kendall. "When are you going to get him started?"

"After he reads over my notes, probably. And he's promised to be fair-minded about my project."

Chloe nodded. "And since he's a Libra, he should be?"

"Yes. He said he would be when I evaluated him and told him he was a Libra. Of course, he called it guessing, but it's more than that, as he'll soon find out. So, I shouldn't have anything to worry about, should I?''

Her roommate didn't answer. Kendall looked over and found Chloe contemplating her sketch. ''You think I have a lot to be worried about, don't you?''

Looking up, Chloe tilted her head and considered Kendall's tense features. ''No, not worried, exactly. Concerned. You have a tendency to worry too much. You're worried about your project and about how you feel about Jared and about what you might dream while you're there. I think you should just let things happen instead of anticipating trouble all the time. You didn't dream about him last night, did you?''

Kendall shook her head. ''No, not that I remember. But it's easier to say relax and don't worry than to actually do it.''

''Make it a personal goal to relax. Worrying won't help at all.''

On that, Kendall was in full agreement. So, keeping all her priorities straight and her problems at a minimum would be her goals for the next two and a half months. It sounded so simple when she thought of it like that, but Kendall knew that nothing was ever as simple as it seemed, and she determined to remain alert to all possibilities of disaster, even if she was going to try not to anticipate them.

The next night, Kendall was ready and waiting in the living room at ten-thirty. Reading a trade journal, she ignored Chloe's comments that it really wasn't fair of Jared to make her work on a Friday night.

''He's working, too, Chloe. Besides, it isn't as if I had other plans.''

"That isn't the point," Chloe argued. "You might have had. He didn't even ask, did he? Did he even suggest that you might have had a date on a Friday night?"

Kendall frowned and worried her thumbnail with her teeth. "No, he didn't. Maybe he thought that if I had other plans I'd mention them."

"Maybe. Of course, since he works in the psych department, maybe he knows you never date, anyway."

"I do so date."

Chloe lifted her head from what she was sewing to give Kendall a pitying look. "When? I've been your roommate for six months and I can only remember your having two dates. Neither of which was repeated."

Shrugging, Kendall flipped a page in her magazine and pretended to study words she didn't really see. "I just didn't have anything in common with them. Besides, I've been busy."

"I don't think you've been too busy," Chloe said slowly. "But it's true that you didn't have anything in common with them."

"I know you're concerned about my love life, Chloe, but believe, me, I'm all right. I go out when I want to, and right now there isn't anybody I *want* to date."

The knock on the door caught her off guard, and Kendall scrambled to her feet, unconsciously glancing in the small mirror beside the front door before her hand reached out to grasp the knob.

"You'd better check your nose while you're at it. I think it just grew a few inches."

With that, Chloe sailed from the room and a frowning Kendall pulled the door open.

"Uh-oh, what's wrong?"

Looking up at Jared's wary expression, Kendall shook her head. "Nothing. Why?" Stepping back, she let him in and went to get her backpack and coat.

"Maybe it was just my imagination, but I thought you looked... rather disconcerted just now."

Disconcerted. That, too, Kendall thought. "I have a roommate with a sick sense of humor."

Jared waited, but Kendall didn't offer anything further. "Where is Chloe? Did she have a date?"

Peeved that Jared had remembered that Chloe was engaged and probably had a date, but hadn't thought that she also might have had one, Kendall found herself struggling to unclench her teeth. "No," she said loudly, so that Chloe could hear her in the kitchen. "Chloe doesn't have a date this evening. Brice is out of town, and she's staying home this evening with Boris and watching reruns of sitcoms."

Laughter could be heard from the kitchen, but Chloe didn't say anything. Kendall, unable to keep herself from seeing the humor in the situation, laughed with her.

"I missed something here, didn't I?"

"Not really," Kendall said as she opened the door. "Just a little roommate routine we have."

They didn't say much on the walk to the lab, and Kendall held on to a strap of her backpack to keep her hand from brushing Jared's.

Larry was waiting for them this time, sitting behind the desk, his feet propped up, eating a taco and watching the far left monitor.

"Mrs. Donlevy is all settled in?" Jared asked.

Larry nodded and swallowed his mouthful of taco. "Got here about twenty minutes ago. Told me she had a can of Mace in case I forgot myself."

Jared's laugh was rather like a snort, and Kendall's eyes went to the monitor as she took off her coat and hung it on the rack. There, in a bedroom decorated in peaches and cream, was a rather pudgy woman who looked to be about sixty-five or seventy. Her hair was wrapped in orange sponge curlers and she was wearing a long flannel nightgown.

Kendall smiled. "So that's the type of woman you prefer, Larry. Many of us in the department have wondered."

"Watch it, Kendall," Larry warned. "I'll soon have access to your dreams. Should they prove embarrassing, I'm not above blackmail."

Relieved to see Larry and grateful for the opportunity to joke with him to keep her mind off Jared's nearness, Kendall also knew that he wasn't serious and that she and her dreams were perfectly safe. "Nothing in my dreams could ever be as potentially damaging as the image of you and Mrs. Donlevy sharing a moment of passion."

Pretending to choke on his food, Larry held up one hand. "Please, not while I'm eating."

Jared placed a hand on Kendall's back and urged her toward the same bedroom she'd occupied before. Feeling her skin burning where his hand rested, Kendall increased her pace to outdistance his hand. She knew he would be able to feel how hot her skin had become. But Jared just kept pace with her, and his hand remained on the small of her back.

He opened the door and Kendall walked quickly into the room. She dropped her pack on the floor and headed for the nightstand, where she pulled out the clipboard and began jotting down what she'd eaten for dinner.

When she got to the emotional-disposition question, Kendall just stared at it for a second. For most of the day she had been fairly relaxed, so she wrote that down. She'd been unable to go the entire day without thinking about Jared and the fact that she was going to see him again, but she didn't go into that at all.

Slightly anxious, she wrote. If he asked, she could say she was worried about getting all the evaluations back that she needed, which was true. Then she wrote: *preoccupied.* That was honest, although she wouldn't tell him precisely what or whom she'd been preoccupied with.

Tearing off the top sheet, she handed it to him and replaced the clipboard in the nightstand. Jared took the form and folded it without reading it. She couldn't help looking up into his face. His expression was calm, yet Kendall knew instinctively that he was feeling anything but. Whether he was hiding his amusement or his anger or whatever else, Kendall suddenly wanted to know what it was. But she didn't feel comfortable actually asking.

"Well," he said, backing toward the door, "I guess I'll go and let you—"

"Wait!" Kendall burst out, suddenly remembering something. "I brought some of my research notes for you to look over this weekend. You should become familiar with what I'm trying to do."

Jared nodded once. "Right."

Kendall pulled the sheaf of papers out of her pack and handed them to him. "That's the outline and a general overview. Will you have time for it this weekend?"

"I'll make time," he said. "I may not have the confidence in astrology and its possible clinical applications that you do, Kendall, but I promised to keep an open mind, and I will."

Wondering why he seemed so distant and...formal, Kendall followed suit. "I know. Thank you."

He nodded and then left. Kendall looked at the door for a moment, then turned around to begin her preparations for bed.

"You got Kendall all tucked in?"

Jared scowled at Larry's flippant remark. "No, she was just filling this out." He held up the form.

Larry squinted, then nodded and plucked the form from Jared's fingers. "Uh-huh. And what did Dr. Arden have for dinner? A hamburger, fries and a soda. Doesn't she know junk food is fattening?"

"It doesn't seem to be something she has to worry about," Jared thought out loud.

Grunting his agreement, Larry looked up at Jared. "Yeah, she's got a great bod. Too bad she isn't willing to share it."

This gained Jared's undivided attention. "Is she stingy with her affections?"

Larry sucked on the straw stuck in his paper cup of soda. "Stingy isn't the word. More like miserly, from what I've heard. A couple of the single professors live in my apartment building. According to them, a few of them have asked her to go out with them, but they struck out. Most of them don't bother. Apparently she treats them like her brothers. Very damaging to the ego, you know. Although Sharon Milburn did see her at a restaurant with a guy once, but no one knows who he was. That was before Christmas."

"The graduate-student grapevine is much more sophisticated now than when I was in school," Jared commented.

"Oh, sure. We have to amuse ourselves, don't we? Some people think she only dates men outside of school, but since she's never mentioned anyone, and since that guy she

was with wasn't from CSU—at least to Sharon's knowledge—then it may be true. Don't know what she could
have against us since we're an intelligent, not to mention
virile, lot.''

"Larry, shut up."

The younger man just waved at him. "Yeah, yeah, I
know I should have more respect, but I, for one, am of a
curious nature. Maybe she was in love with that guy and
hasn't gotten over him. Sure would explain a lot.''

Not wanting to give that theory any more latitude than
Larry's other ideas, Jared stole one of his assistant's tacos
and ordered him out of his chair. "Go sit in your own hard
little chair," he said.

Larry got up and moved, grumbling every step of the
way. "If I'd known you weren't going to let me push you
around, I never would have taken this job."

Shaking his head at the absurdity that was Larry, Jared
glanced at the television monitors. Mrs. Donlevy was
asleep and Kendall was just getting into bed. She was
wearing the same little cotton nightdress. She probably
thought it wasn't provocative, Jared thought ruefully.

"You know," Larry went on, "Kendall knows that we're
a couple of single men who have to sit up all night and
watch television monitors showing people sleeping. The
very least she could have done was wear a see-through
negligee."

Jared agreed, but merely pointed to the other monitor.
"Mrs. Donlevy just entered REM."

Larry scrambled to adjust his monitor and camera angles. Jared looked back at Kendall, who was snuggled into
bed and reading the books and notes scattered around her.
He picked up the form Larry had left on the desk and
scanned it. Fairly relaxed, slightly anxious, and preoccupied. What about? he wondered.

He had to admit that on and off all day he had been rather preoccupied with thoughts of Kendall. The anticipation of seeing her again had been stronger than he would have thought. And it wasn't as if she was trying to get his attention.

"She's snoring again," Larry grumbled. "Next time, why don't you watch Mrs. Donlevy and I'll watch Kendall Arden."

Jared chuckled. "Forget it. Mrs. Donlevy and her snoring are yours until the end of April."

"I guess that means Kendall is yours?"

Kendall chose that moment to close her books and turn off her lamp. Jared ignored Larry and adjusted his monitoring instruments. But ignoring the man and ignoring his words were distinctly different propositions. The thought of Kendall being his sent swift pulses of heat through his blood, settling uncomfortably in a most sensitive area.

Berating himself for his wandering thoughts, he rose and crossed to the file cabinet to retrieve the file that bore Kendall Arden's name.

Jared was glad that Larry was working tonight. Instead of just watching Kendall and thinking things he shouldn't, maybe he and Larry could have a few distracting conversations.

Mrs. Donlevy chose that moment to let loose another loud snore. Jared chuckled as Larry groaned.

The grass was green and thick and soft, and smelled as though it had been freshly cut. There were several trees scattered around and a small lake or pond was only a few feet from where she stood.

The other side of the pond was hazy, as was the sky. She couldn't quite make out the tops of the trees. Then she was walking to the pond's edge. The sunlight felt delicious on her naked skin.

Naked? Kendall looked down and saw that she was, indeed, naked. She glanced around, but there seemed to be no one else to see her, so she stretched and walked into the slightly cool water of the pond.

She swam at a leisurely pace until she suddenly felt the water change. She stopped swimming and began to tread water. There, just ahead of her, was a whirlpool. Its edge was only inches from her bobbing body. She felt its current tugging on her legs, and she tried to pull away, but couldn't. It was pulling her into its whirling center.

Fear clasped her heart, and she knew she was going to drown. Then strong arms enfolded her from behind, and she was pulled away from the whirlpool.

Kendall knew whom the arms belonged to, and she wasn't even embarrassed at having been caught swimming naked. She only felt sensual pleasure at being held close to his naked body, his strong arm under her breasts.

Stopping in waist-deep water, Kendall turned in his arms and looked up into Jared's eyes. They were as dark as ever, and familiar, but now they burned with a desire Kendall had never seen, but suspected—hoped—had existed.

He was going to kiss her now, she thought, and she smiled. His head lowered and when their lips touched, she knew she was dreaming. She knew, but she didn't care. She'd never felt so beautiful or so wanted. And she wanted him, too.

It had to be a dream, she thought, because she'd never felt this kind of totally engulfing passion and doubted that it existed outside the fantasy of dreams. That's why she resisted the pull of consciousness.

Let me make love with him before I wake up, she told herself, as she felt his hands sliding over her body. *His lips were incredible... masterful... and suddenly... gone.*

Chapter Five

Kendall didn't want to be awake, yet she was. Her eyes blinked open to the darkness of the room. Her breathing was erratic, as was her heartbeat. What an incredible dream. It had been really erotic and now—

"Kendall?"

Jared. Oh, no, she thought frantically. How can I ever face him again?

"Kendall? Do you remember any of the dream you just woke from?"

Taking a deep breath, Kendall tried to figure out what she should say, but her mind was still filled with images of her body entwined with Jared's.

"Kendall?"

She had to tell him something. "I...uh...only images, really. There was a big grassy area and a pond. It was fuzzy looking. I could feel the sunlight, but I'm not sure if I really saw the sun, though."

At least all of that was true.

"Okay. What were you doing?"

It was eerie for Kendall to lie there in the dark and listen to Jared's voice, knowing he wasn't really standing next to her but was in the next room. "Uh, I was swimming. And there was a whirlpool that I almost got sucked into."

"Almost? What happened?"

"I was a few inches from it and it was pulling me in, but . . . someone . . . pulled me away."

That was true.

"Did you see who it was?"

"No, he was behind me."

She was starting to fudge things a little now. *Please don't ask me anymore questions,* she thought.

"So, it was a man. Did you know him?"

"I don't think so," she lied.

"Could you describe him?"

"Not really. He was tall and muscular and could swim well."

Not even for the sake of science would Kendall tell Jared what had really happened in that dream. And she didn't think she would ever have to worry about forgetting it, either, for the images were burned into her memory.

"Do you remember anything else?"

Like the fact that I was naked and you were naked and we were about to make love and it was feeling fantastic? "No, nothing really."

"Okay. It's seven-forty, by the way."

Kendall nodded in the dark, knowing that he could still see her via his infrared camera. She took a few deep breaths and reached over to flip on the light. Dragging herself from the bed, she made her way quickly to the bathroom. Under the shower she tried to ignore the way her body had become highly sensitized—and all because of a dream! Added to that was the fact that she'd realized that it was a dream before it was over. She could remember knowing that she was dreaming, but not wanting it to end. Why was that?

Turning off the shower, she reached for a towel and began rubbing herself briskly. She'd known it was a dream, she reasoned, because it had been too good to be true. She could just imagine Chloe's reaction. She'd probably wonder if the dream had been precognitive. Ha! Jared Dalton feeling that kind of passion for Kendall Arden? Talk about the *reverse* of precognition!

After drying her hair and getting dressed, she opened the door of the bedroom and found the office next to it empty. Glancing around, she noticed that there was a note taped to the door to Jared's office.

Gone to get food. Be right back. J.

While she was debating about whether she should write a note and leave, she heard the side door open and turned to see Jared coming in with bags of food.

"You don't need to keep feeding me, you know," she said. "I could just go home and get something."

Jared's eyes seemed to bore into hers, and Kendall felt as if he was trying to read her mind. She looked away. If she gazed into those dark eyes too much, she was sure he'd see the truth of that dream.

"I know I don't have to. But I hate eating alone, don't you?"

Kendall shrugged. "I guess so. Where's Larry?"

"I let him go home. Mrs. Donlevy was up at six and gone by six-thirty, so there was no reason for him to hang around."

Why did the room suddenly seem smaller now that Kendall knew that they were alone and wouldn't be interrupted? She sank into the chair beside the desk and hoped Jared couldn't hear the deafening sound of her heartbeat.

"So, what do you do if there are three people here at once? Or doesn't that happen?"

Jared sat down and started taking the food out of the bags. "Yes, there are times when there are three subjects here at one time. But not often. We just have to be a bit more alert in watching the monitors. Since a lot of the research is dependent on our trusting the subjects to relate their dreams whenever they awake and remember them, it isn't too hard to keep the notes we need."

Guilt kept Kendall from looking Jared in the eye. But even massive doses of guilt wouldn't be enough to drag the details of that dream from her. Maybe she'd write it down and mail it to him after her part in his experiment had been completed.

Their conversation over breakfast was minimal and not in the least personal. Kendall was still reeling from her feelings her dream had evoked and Jared seemed preoccupied.

He was probably trying to work out some problem in his experiment, she thought, and he was also probably wishing she would leave. Finishing her juice, Kendall abruptly stood and cleared her throat. "I really should be leaving."

Jared's dark brown eyes blinked up at her. He looked rather startled. "You should? I'm sorry, I didn't mean to keep you. I didn't realize you might have somewhere to be so early on a Saturday morning."

Now it was Kendall's turn to look surprised. "Well, actually, I don't. But I didn't want to keep you from your work."

Jared smiled and Kendall's stomach flip-flopped accordingly. "I don't usually work on Saturday mornings," he said. "Or Sunday, either."

"Oh."

Kendall nodded a few times as she sidled around Jared to the coatrack. Her lightweight ski jacket suddenly felt heavy as she struggled into it. When she turned toward the door, she discovered Jared standing beside the door to his office, watching her.

"Uh, should I come back on Monday night?"

Jared nodded. "I'll pick you up."

About to object, Kendall saw that the neutral expression of his face wasn't reflected in his eyes. There was stubbornness and a sense of determination there, and she wasn't up to fighting it. Kendall was having enough trouble with her own feelings. She didn't have the stamina to take on a will as strong as she suspected Jared's was.

"All right," she said, and turned to open the door. Just as her hand touched the knob, she remembered that her backpack was still in the bedroom. Turning abruptly to retrace her steps, she bumped her nose on the solid wall that was Jared's chest.

A startled gasp escaped her lips as she realized that Jared must have been right behind her. Her eyes slipped up his body and her embarrassed smile died when her eyes met his.

She'd only seen that expression once before—and it had been in her dream. It was desire.

Kendall decided she must be imagining things. She was confusing her dream with reality. Then he reached out and smoothed his fingers over her cheek, and Kendall knew that it wasn't a dream. Her skin burned along the path his fingers took from her cheek to her neck, where his hand rested warmly just below her ear, his thumb idly stroking her earlobe.

He was going to kiss her. Kendall could see his intention mirrored in his eyes. And she shouldn't let him. She should break away and tell him she didn't want this.

Yet she couldn't move. She *did* want it, but she was afraid of what it would mean.

"You shouldn't," she whispered, appalled at how inviting her own voice sounded to her ears.

Jared's eyes continued to devour her face. A fleeting expression of bemusement danced across his features and then was gone. Left behind was only desire. "I have to," he uttered as his head descended.

The first touch of his lips on hers was feathery and teasing. It was enough, though, to cause Kendall to gasp with pleasure. His lips then settled over her slightly parted mouth and Kendall was lost.

Never had she experienced such overwhelming emotions from a kiss. Except in her dream, she thought distantly. It occurred to her that this might be another dream, but she didn't care. If it is, don't wake me, she pleaded.

Her arms found their way under his open lab coat to wrap around his lean waist, and she pulled him closer so that her body touched his from thigh to chest. Kendall had never cared one way or the other about her height before, but now she was so glad she was tall, because her five foot seven inches fit perfectly against Jared's six-foot frame.

Finally pulling his lips from hers, Jared then kissed the bridge of her nose and her eyes and her forehead and her cheeks. "I've been wanting to do this for days."

His lips were now nibbling her earlobe and Kendall tilted her head to accommodate him. Her eyes floated half-open to gaze fuzzily around her. Although it wasn't a green meadow with a lovely pond, she was feeling exactly the same. Then her eyes focused and she recognized Jared's lab. She knew that she wasn't in the midst of a dream— that she was standing in his lab kissing and being kissed. This was Jared and she worked with Jared every day.

Jared couldn't help noticing the sudden stiffening of her body, and he pulled back to look at her now pinched features. "Kendall? What is it? What's wrong?"

Kendall refused to let her emotions have free rein and she fought the tears that threatened. Losing control of herself wasn't something that happened to her—in fact, it *never* happened. And she couldn't afford to be weak now. She let her arms fall to her sides and stepped out of Jared's embrace. "I'm sorry," she said as calmly as she could manage.

"Why? What's wrong?"

"This is," she said, waving her hand between them. "It shouldn't have happened. And it won't happen again."

With that she walked around him and into the bedroom to retrieve her pack. The prospect of a clean getaway was squashed when she saw Jared blocking the doorway.

"Would you mind explaining what you just said?"

Kendall considered telling him that, yes, she did mind, but she doubted he would be satisfied with that answer. Unable to meet his probing eyes, she directed her words to his neck. "I don't think it needs explanation. It shouldn't have happened. I think we should both try to forget it ever *did* happen."

Her eyes drifted of their own volition up to collide with his. She'd expected anger, perhaps, or mocking derision. But not ambivalence. He looked as though he wanted to disagree with her, but couldn't.

"Do you think that's possible? Forgetting it, I mean? It was rather...amazing, wasn't it?"

Kendall blushed to the roots of her red-gold hair. He's perfectly serious, she thought. "That's beside the point," she contended.

"And the point is?"

Now he was being deliberately obtuse. "The point is that you and I work together here and I don't get involved with coworkers."

Jared turned away and sighed before looking back at her determined expression. "I suppose this is an important rule to you?"

If he only knew, Kendall thought. "Yes, it's very important. And since you understand, I'm sure that we can put this behind us and not let it affect our working relationship."

"Well, we can try," Jared said.

It wasn't a very convincing response, Kendall thought, but it was better than a few others she could think of. "Fine," she said firmly. "If you could read the notes I left with you over the weekend, I'd appreciate any comments. And I'll see you Monday."

He nodded. "Ten-thirty?"

"That's fine."

Kendall edged her way to the door then, wary that he might try to stop her again, but he just waved once and turned toward the desk. Kendall fairly flew out the door and up the steps to the deserted main hall of the building.

Making her way to the main doors, she let herself out into the bright Saturday morning sunshine. It was still cold, being the last of February, but the sun should have been warming. Unfortunately Kendall was frozen from the inside out. She'd put her emotions on ice because it was the only way she could deal with them.

She turned toward the post office and was grateful it was open until noon on Saturdays. Her box was stuffed with returned surveys, and Kendall noted that they should give her more than enough to begin the final phase of her project. Her lack of enthusiasm over this only made her more determined than ever to forget about Jared Dalton and his sizzling kisses.

Jared, on the other hand, had no intentions of forgetting one detail of what they'd shared. Locked in his memory were images of the softness of Kendall's skin, the desire in Kendall's eyes, and the hesitant passion in Kendall's kisses.

No, forgetting what had happened was not Jared's problem. Keeping his hands off her the next time he saw her was his problem. But more challenging was trying to figure out a way to get Kendall to forego this rule of hers just this once.

Mulling possible solutions over in his head, Jared walked around the lab and made sure all the instruments and monitors were turned off and that all the personal files and videotapes were locked away. Then he gathered his briefcase, dropped Kendall's research notes in it, grabbed his coat and left.

His sports car was the only vehicle in the faculty parking lot, and he smiled ruefully as he made his way toward the gleaming dark blue machine. Many women had been impressed by this car, he thought. But he doubted Kendall would be. He liked the car—love was probably a better word—and he took pride in it, but he had already figured out that it would take much more than a slick car and his own looks and charm to sway Kendall Arden from her rule about coworkers.

All the way home, Jared considered and discarded ideas until, by the time he pulled into his driveway and let himself in, he was at a loss.

A screech, followed by some whistles greeted him. "Good morning, Harpo," he said to the cockatoo. Harpo danced sideways on his perch and blinked at Jared. The cockatoo's dark pink coloring had thrown Jared off when he'd first been presented with the bird, but now he was used to him.

"Harpo, it's too bad you can't talk, because I need some advice. I know this woman, see, and she's beautiful and intelligent, with a body that's...well..." Jared's wolf whistle was soft and low.

Harpo danced on his perch and let out a high-pitched fast imitation of the whistle. Jared's head jerked around. Then he laughed. "You got it, pal. Anyway—" Suddenly he paused and frowned. "Why didn't I notice her last semester? She started working here in September. I mean, I know I've seen her at faculty meetings, but she never said anything or brought attention to herself.

"And she always sat in the back, near the door. It was almost as though she was avoiding—"

Harpo whistled again and Jared smiled. "This might be an interesting theory, Harpo, old buddy."

Jared fell silent, staring out the front window of his house and ruminating on Kendall's odd behavior before this past week and since. He remembered the desire in her eyes that day in the lecture room and again this morning. Maybe her rule about not dating coworkers was keeping Dr. Kendall Arden from going after something she wanted.

Harpo let out another screech and a few more whistles, including his new wolf whistle. Jared smiled. "You were right the first time, Harpo. Kendall is a sexy number."

Turning toward the kitchen, Jared looked back at the cockatoo. "Sorry, pal, I almost forgot to feed you, didn't I? Kendall—" Harpo whistled again and Jared laughed. "That's right, Kendall's the sexy number. And the sexy ones can make you forget all about feeding yourself, much less your faithful bird."

Jared left the room and Harpo cocked his head, his whitish crest flapping slightly. Then he whistled loudly and screeched.

"You look weird. What happened?"

Kendall closed the front door behind her and turned around to face Chloe, who was sitting in front of the television, watching cartoons.

"And good morning to you, too, Chloe."

"Good morning, Kendall," Chloe said. "You still look weird. What happened?"

Kendall opened the closet door and hung up her coat before returning to the living room and sitting on the other end of the sofa from Chloe. Boris jumped up and demanded a compulsory pat and then left.

"I'm waiting," Chloe sang.

"Why did something have to happen? Can't I just look weird and still have people accept me?"

"No, you can't. What happened?"

"Nothing, really. Look, I got a lot more surveys. I think I have enough now."

Chloe wasn't buying it. "What happened? He made a pass at you, didn't he?"

Kendall wondered if that kiss could be construed as a pass. She didn't think so. Slumping into the soft cushions of the sofa, she murmured, "He kissed me."

"Oh." Chloe sounded disappointed. "So, he kissed you." She shrugged. "Only once?"

Kendall sat up straight. "What do you mean, 'only once?' This wasn't just a peck on the cheek, I'll have you know. This was a reach-down-inside-you-and-ricochet-off-your-nerve-endings kiss. This was a burn-your-insides, singe-your-eyelashes-off kiss."

Chloe blinked at her. "So. You liked it."

"I loved it," Kendall said despairingly. "And I told him it could never happen again."

"Uh-huh. And what did he say?"

"He agreed with me," Kendall said. "I think."

"You know, Kendall, it might be time to rethink your stance on this rule about dating coworkers. I, personally, think that Jared Dalton is too good a catch to be thrown back."

Kendall slumped back into the cushions. "I wasn't trying to catch him. And I'm afraid that if I started seeing him that it would prove disastrous. It just isn't the right time or place."

"Time and tide and affairs of the heart wait for no man—or woman, for that matter. Especially not when you spend as much time together as you two will these next few months."

Kendall dropped her face into her hands. "Why couldn't he have been old and fat and ugly?"

"Come on, cheer up. So you bend a few rules on the road to romance and success. Who'll know?"

"I will."

"Oh. Well, then, as depressing as it sounds, maybe you're right. In the meantime, come over and watch cartoons with me."

Kendall laughed as they watched the cartoon antics and she was grateful to have Chloe as a friend. Her problems were still there, but they seemed more bearable with someone who not only listened, but made her laugh.

To Kendall's relief, Chloe didn't mention Jared again that weekend, and although Kendall wanted to immerse herself in her survey and begin her evaluations, she also had a test to give on Monday morning, so most of the weekend was spent preparing that.

She tried to put visions of Jared and that kiss from her mind, but they crept back in when she wasn't on guard. And in her most unguarded moment, when she was asleep, she dreamed of him again.

She dreamed that they were riding in a sports car and that he was kissing her. More than kissing, really, they were necking. But the car was still moving. Waking up, Kendall decided that one was too weird to be precognitive, since no one would drive a car that fast and make out at the same time.

Nevertheless, she wrote the dream down in the dream journal she'd begun keeping. She wasn't in the lab, so she really wasn't obligated to do it, but since she wasn't exactly being the model subject Jared deserved, she figured that the least she could do was supply him with all her dreams once she didn't have to see him every day....

During the next two weeks, Kendall was kept almost too busy to think about Jared and the kiss they'd shared. It was the two weeks prior to spring break, and consequently she had papers due from her students in both her classes and tests to give in both her labs. She spent a lot of time talking to those students outside of class and answering their questions.

They weren't left alone in Jared's lab at all. Larry was always there when she arrived and he was there when she awoke. Kendall couldn't decide if she was grateful or resentful of his presence.

It was taking Kendall longer and longer to fall asleep, though. After the first dream she'd had of herself and Jared, and then the one she'd had at home, she was afraid it would happen again. Even when she didn't dream of him, though, the dreams she did have were weird enough, many with strange images and unrelated circumstances in them.

Kendall knew that during those two weeks Jared had begun to introduce outside stimuli during sleep to induce certain types of dreams. Although she didn't know exactly when he'd started it, she knew it was being done when she dreamed she was surfing, and then dreamed she was snorkeling—both in one night. They had played tapes of water dripping or running, and consequently she had dreamed of water.

The last session before spring break must have been transportation night, because Kendall dreamed she was on the Orient Express. Jared was the conductor and kept showing up, kissing her and leaving. When Kendall woke up, she described the dream in detail, except that Jared was now an unknown man.

After she finished her description of the dream, she waited in the dark, listening for his familiar voice to wish her a good morning. It was a ritual that Kendall had come to look forward to.

This morning, however, she was unpleasantly surprised.

"Rise and shine, Doc."

Kendall groaned. "Go away, Larry."

"Heh, heh, heh. Come on, move your bee-hind out of that bed. It is now eight-oh-six. And if I'm not mistaken, you have a class to teach at nine."

"Oh, no."

"Oh, yes."

"Why didn't Jared wake me?" She demanded as she scrambled out of bed without bothering to turn on the lamp. By now she knew her way to the bathroom in the dark quite well.

"Because we don't wake people who are dreaming. And that last one of yours went on for almost forty-five minutes. Very close to a record, but Mrs. Donlevy has you beat by four minutes."

"That must have been the dream where she made you her love slave," Kendall mocked as she shut the bathroom door behind her and turned on the light. She could hear Larry's voice raised in umbrage, but she just turned on the shower. She did have a class at nine, and she had to hurry.

Emerging from the bedroom at quarter to nine, Kendall found Larry eating cold pizza and drinking warm soda. It was the first time she hadn't seen Jared there.

"Where is Jared?"

"He got a phone call and left to talk to Dr. Grady."

"What's going on?"

Larry shrugged. "I don't know. But I gathered it was personal. Sorry about the change in your routine. I know he always handles your case and his voice is the first thing you hear in the morning, but I'm sure you'll agree that my dulcet tones are a remarkable improvement."

Kendall rolled her eyes and made her way toward the door. "Maybe you should go over to the drama department and take a few elocution classes, Larry. Perhaps then you wouldn't frighten women when they hear your voice first thing in the morning."

"Ha! I'll have you know—"

"Sorry to miss what would have been a stimulating discussion, I'm sure, but I have to get to my class."

She left then, hurrying up the steps and wishing she had the time to pop into the office and see if Millie knew what was going on with Jared. She hoped it wasn't an illness in his family or something.

She bypassed the office and continued up the stairs to the classroom, where she barely made it by nine.

An hour later she gathered her materials and left. She headed for the office first, hoping maybe Jared had left her a note, although she couldn't imagine why he would. Millie looked relieved to see her.

"I've been trying to find out where you were."

Kendall's eyes widened. "Me? I've been teaching a class. It's on my schedule. What happened with—"

Millie raised her hand. "I should have known that. Oh, well, no time now. Dr. Dalton needs to see you in the lab."

Taken aback, Kendall just said, "Oh."

"Don't look so worried," Millie told her. "It isn't bad news."

"Oh, good," Kendall managed and backed out of the office. She still had no idea what was going on, but she made her way down to his office, her curiosity overcoming her apprehension.

His office door was closed and Kendall knocked twice. The door was flung open almost immediately and Jared stood there with a scowl on his face. "Good, come here."

He reached out and wrapped his hand around her wrist, then pulled her into his office. "Larry said you got a phone call and had to leave. Then Millie said you wanted to see me," she said as he shut the door.

"Right. Thanks for coming down so quickly. Listen, could you come stay at my house for a few days?"

Chapter Six

"I beg your pardon?"

Kendall was sure that she'd misunderstood him. Yet the thought that she hadn't sent alternating shafts of excitement and dread through her.

Jared apparently didn't notice the wariness in her wide gray eyes. He turned away after shutting the door and dropped into his chair. "I have to go to Baltimore for the weekend, and I was hoping you could stay at my house while I'm gone."

"Oh," Kendall said, wondering why she didn't feel more relieved. "Nothing's wrong, I hope."

"Wrong? Oh, you mean bad news? No, no one's sick or dead or anything. Although I could kill my cousin for doing this."

"Your cousin?"

Jared grimaced. "Yes. My cousin Artie. The one who gave me the cockatoo for Christmas. He called me this morning and told me to come home right away. Then, after scaring the you-know-what out of me, he tells me he's getting married and I have to be his best man.''

"Isn't this rather short notice for a wedding?"

Jared ran a hand exasperatedly through his dark hair. "For normal people, yes. For Artie, no. And since we promised each other years ago that if we ever got married we'd be the other's best man, I can't get out of it."

Kendall nodded absently as she watched Jared stuff some papers into his briefcase. "Would you want to get out of it?"

He stopped and grinned, sitting down behind his desk and shutting his case. "Not really. I don't know if you've ever been to an Irish wedding or an Irish wake, or any other Irish gathering, but one thing they never are is dull."

Now that she thought about it, Kendall realized that Jared did look rather Irish—black Irish—with his dark eyes and hair. She'd never thought about it before, and she still didn't see why any of this was a problem that should involve her. "It sounds like a good time, but what has all this to do with my staying at your house? You'll only be gone for two days, right? If it's the project, I'm sure that Larry—"

"Larry is going to Myrtle Beach for the weekend. He couldn't leave for the entire week of spring break, so I gave him a four-day weekend. He left about an hour ago. I'm not worried about the project, though, since nothing is scheduled on weekends, anyway. Tonight's sessions are the only ones I'll have to reschedule, and you and Mrs. Donlevy are the only subjects. I've already called and rescheduled her. An extra day next week isn't going to inconvenience you too much, is it?"

Kendall shook her head. "No, of course not, but I still don't see the problem ... Why do you want me to stay at your house?"

Sighing, Jared leaned back and looked at her. "The problem is Harpo."

"Harpo?"

"My cockatoo. I've only had him since Christmas, and I don't think he's totally comfortable yet. At least I don't think he's comfortable enough to be left in the house for that long by himself."

His bird? "How do you know he isn't comfortable?"

"For one thing, he doesn't talk. He just whistles. According to a bird book I read, he should have learned to talk by now. And sometimes, if I leave him alone too long, he tears holes in the furniture. Not big holes, but I shudder to think what he'd do if I left him for a whole weekend. My living room set is new. Besides, he needs to be fed and watered every day, too. I was going to ask my part-time housekeeper to come in, but she went to visit relatives this weekend."

Now Kendall was beginning to get the point of this conversation. "Doesn't Harpo have a cage?"

Jared nodded sheepishly. "Yes. A huge one. But he always looks so depressed in there. Like he's serving time for a crime he didn't commit. So I got him a tree."

"A tree?" Kendall gaped.

"Not a big tree. An indoor sort of tree. It's a jungle tree. He likes the branches better than artificial perches."

Kendall wanted to laugh at Jared's pampering of a bird. But when she considered some of the things she and Chloe did for Boris, she didn't. But neither did she think she could spend the weekend at his house, even if he wasn't going to be there.

"Jared, I don't think I should—"

"Come on, Kendall. I wouldn't ask if it weren't necessary. Everybody I know who could have taken care of him is leaving town during spring break. You're staying here all weekend, aren't you?"

"Well, yes, but why would I have to stay at your house? Couldn't I just drop by once a day and check on Harpo?"

Jared nodded. "Yes. But I got the impression you didn't have a car."

Kendall shook her head. "I don't. But why should that matter?"

"Because I live about ten miles outside town and the buses don't run out there. If you were there most of the time, Harpo wouldn't get lonely and take it out on my new furniture. I'd leave you my car if I weren't driving it down to Baltimore for the wedding."

Thinking of Jared's sleek new car, which she'd seen several times in the parking lot, Kendall was convinced of his sincerity. No man would let a woman he didn't know very well drive a car like that unless it was unavoidable.

"Well, I guess I could do it," she agreed without much enthusiasm. "If I really needed anything, Chloe could drive out."

"Great." Jared smiled, and Kendall was uncomfortably aware that if Jared continued to smile at her like that, she would agree to do almost anything for him. But she didn't have time to dwell on what any of those things might be, because Jared was forging ahead.

"I have to do a few things around here, and then I have to go home and pack and leave. Artie's bachelor party is tonight at seven-thirty. And I have to hunt down some food and entertainment on short notice. Can you be ready by noon?"

Kendall looked at her watch, not wanting to think about what sort of entertainment Jared would be getting for his cousin's bachelor party. "I guess so. I only have one lab to teach today, and that's in about twenty minutes. After that I'm free, but remember, I have to pack when I get home.''

"Twelve-thirty?"

He obviously wasn't expecting her to take much. Of course, for two and a half days, Kendall didn't suppose she'd need much. So she nodded. "All right. But I think you should know that I don't know much about cockatoos.''

Jared just winked. ''That's all right. Harpo doesn't know much about beautiful women.''

At a few minutes before one, Jared pulled into a graveled drive in a slightly wooded area near the Susquehanna River. The house was tucked under a canopy of trees that let sunlight dapple through to create dancing patterns on the sloping roof. To Kendall, it seemed like a vacation cottage in paradise.

''What do you think?''

Looking through the windshield of the car, Kendall waited for Jared to stop and turn off the ignition. Then she glanced at him. She had been nervous for the whole ride, remembering the dream she'd had about them that had taken place in this vehicle. But now that they'd stopped, she could breathe easier. Since the car wasn't moving now, her dream hadn't become reality. With a sigh of relief, she looked at the house and its wooded surroundings.

''It's beautiful,'' she declared sincerely, marveling at the serenity around her. ''Are you sure you don't need me to stay for longer than three days?''

She meant her question as a joke, but the second it was out of her mouth and she saw the way Jared's eyes widened, then darkened with desire, she realized that her joke had backfired. Kendall sat mesmerized for a minute, then felt her throat go dry. She began groping for the door handle.

Jared reached out and grasped her hand. "Don't run, Kendall. I won't hurt you."

Forcing herself to meet his steady gaze, Kendall saw that he was serious. "I know that you think you wouldn't. That you wouldn't intend to."

"That's all any of us can promise, isn't it?"

Kendall frowned. Trying to think while Jared was holding her hand and stroking her wrist and sitting so close was nearly impossible. When his other hand came to rest on her shoulder, she told herself that she really should move away, that she should put at least several feet of air between herself and Jared. Then he was leaning toward her and Kendall just sighed and lifted her face to receive his kiss.

Knowing what the touch of his lips to hers did to her nervous system didn't help prepare Kendall. She was instantly lost in the sensations that rippled through her. Jared's lips slid over hers and his tongue urged her to open her mouth, which she did with practically no hesitation.

For something that was supposed to be so wrong for her, Kendall couldn't help but think how right she felt with Jared. They both strained to get closer, but the confines of the sports car barred that. It was her dream, she thought fuzzily. It was coming true. Except that the car wasn't moving. Not that it mattered to Kendall, since she felt as though she was racing ahead full speed emotionally, if not physically.

Kendall's hands crept up over Jared's arms and shoulders. One rested on the side of his neck, the other tangled in his longish hair. It was curling over his collar now and Kendall loved the feel of it winding around her fingers.

She wasn't aware of where Jared's hands were until she felt the hand that was on her shoulder slip down toward

her waist, where his other hand was. But as his hand slid
down, so did the zipper to her ski jacket. She didn't even
notice his hand nudging her coat aside, but her whole body
jerked with surprise and pleasure when he touched her
breast, his hand lifting and caressing her flesh.

Not able to stop the moan of pleasure that started deep
within her and vibrated against Jared's lips, Kendall
shifted in her seat to give him more access to her body. It
was then that her thigh bumped the gearshift and the car
began to roll.

Neither of them noticed for a few seconds, until they
started to pick up speed. With a shriek Kendall pulled away
and Jared mumbled a few unintelligible phrases as he
scrambled around before managing to apply the brake and
put the car back into park—moments before they would
have hit a tree at the end of the driveway.

Kendall's heart was beating so fast and so hard that she
was sure Jared could hear it. As soon as she could, she
jumped out of the car and walked a few feet away. The
images from her dream had just merged with the reality of
the present, and Kendall was struggling to maintain her
emotional equilibrium.

Jared got out, but stayed on his side of the car, looking
at her over the roof. "You knocked it into neutral," he
explained.

Having already figured that out for herself, Kendall just
zipped up her coat. "I know that."

"Then what's wrong? I thought it was sort of funny."

She looked over at him and saw that he was smiling, but
that there was puzzlement in his eyes, as well. Kicking at a
piece of gravel, Kendall sighed and looked away, staring at
the tree they'd almost hit. What could she say? That she'd
dreamed the whole thing and that it had just come true?
He'd know that she'd dreamed about him, and if he knew

that, a very private part of her would be exposed and vulnerable to a hurt she was too afraid to risk.

She shrugged and forced a smile. "I guess it was funny, but it sort of caught me off guard and frightened me a little."

Jared gazed at her for a moment, then shut the car door. "You're all right, aren't you?"

"I'm fine," Kendall said, feeling stupid now.

"Come on into the house and I'll introduce you to Harpo. I'd like to stay so we could eat lunch together or something, but I really have to get to Baltimore as soon as possible."

Kendall smiled and nodded as she followed him into his house. "I understand."

Kendall was not surprised in the least by the elegant charm of the decor. She'd expected as much from a Libra. They were lovers of beauty and luxury. Not that the house was especially luxurious, she decided, taking in the cream-colored sofa and armchairs and dark brown carpeting and solid oak tables. She imagined that the rest of the house was similarly balanced in color and symmetry.

It was the screechy squawk that was discordant. Turning to fully face the room, Kendall saw that on one wall was a fireplace and in the inside corner of the room stood a large tree, and peeking out from the leaves was a bird.

"He's pink," she said in surprise.

"He's not pink," Jared defended. "He's . . . just light red. Actually he's a roseate, or rose-breasted, cockatoo."

He was that, Kendall thought. His breast was indeed rose colored. Deep pink, in fact. His head was cocked to one side in curiosity and his pinkish gray crest rippled up and down. He looked to be about fifteen inches long, and from the way his short, dark gray legs gripped his perch, Kendall deduced that he was quite strong.

Walking past Jared and seeing the large cage that was apparently unused, Kendall saw that the floor around the tree was covered with fake green grass.

"What's with the Astroturf? Trying to make him think he's still in the jungles of South America?"

"Actually, his species is from Tasmania, but no, the reason that's there is that newspapers look tacky."

Kendall laughed softly. "Only a Libra would install Astroturf to avoid ruining their decor."

Jared scowled. "I doubt that that has anything to do with it. And it does spoil the decor, since it's green. But I haven't been able to find any brown Astroturf."

He's serious, Kendall thought, and she snickered. "If there is such a thing, I have every confidence you will find it."

She shrugged out of her coat and handed it to Jared. As he hung it on a brass coat tree near the front door, a raucous wolf whistle from behind her caused her to spin around in surprise. But all she saw was Harpo, dancing sideways on a branch in his tree and eyeing her.

"Fresh."

Harpo whistled again. Hearing Jared clearing his throat, Kendall looked back at him. "I'm just going to go pack," he said quickly. "Make yourself at home."

Then he disappeared into the hallway. Kendall realized that she'd temporarily forgotten the kiss and her lame excuse for shooting out of the car as if her behind was on fire. Now she remembered and wondered if he realized she'd lied.

Just the knowledge that she had lied, at least by omission, made Kendall want to kick herself. Jared deserved better than her selfish attempts at preserving her pride. What good was pride if you hated yourself for it?

Unable to rise above her own fears, Kendall sighed and wandered around the living room, glancing at the books in the cases that flanked the picture window, then through Jared's record collection, which was pretty extensive.

From there she went into the well-appointed kitchen and noted that nothing was out of place and that there were no dirty dishes in the sink. She opened the refrigerator and found that it was stocked with plenty of food, as were the cupboards. She concluded that Jared must be either an accomplished cook, or his part-time housekeeper also cooked for him. Kendall liked to think that this person was an overweight, middle-aged woman who was married and had six kids.

"Think you'll be able to manage to feed yourself?"

Kendall turned quickly and found Jared watching her. "Umm, I think so. Do you have all this food because you cook or because someone else does?"

"I do, sometimes. But my housekeeper also cooks for me. Mostly casseroles, though, since my schedule is so unpredictable. She thinks I don't eat properly."

Kendall smiled. He looked healthy enough to her. "So, now that I know I can eat, what does Harpo like?"

"Harpo likes to mooch, but don't let him have anything other than his own food, except nuts."

Walking over to a lower cupboard, Jared pulled out a bag of bird food and a bag of mixed nuts, unshelled. "A half cup of his food and some nuts for a treat every day is usually enough. His food and water dishes are in the tree."

Not knowing what else to say, Kendall just stood there. Jared must have seen the uncertainty in her eyes. "We seem to have a problem, don't we, Kendall?"

She knew what he was talking about and didn't even try to pretend ignorance. "Yes, we do. But it shouldn't be one."

"I think that my solution and your solution aren't going to match up."

Somehow, he'd moved while he was talking and was now right in front of her. "There is only one solution," she said, trying to sound firm and failing.

"Ahh, now that's something we really do disagree on." He paused, looking down at her. "I suppose you'd think it a bad idea for me to kiss you goodbye."

"Jared, I have very good reasons for—"

"Yeah, I know. Your rule. But you want to know something, Kendall? Since meeting you, I suddenly find myself wanting to break all the rules."

He kissed her again, and Kendall couldn't muster the strength to pull away. It felt too good. But just as she parted her lips and started to lean into him, he pulled away and grinned. "As much as I am enjoying this, I really do have to leave. And I won't if you continue to look so sexy."

Kendall's eyes flashed when she realized he was making fun of her. "This might not be serious for you, Jared, but I—"

"Believe me, I'm more serious than even I thought I could be. And I'm sorry I can't stay and discuss it further with you," he said, "but I have a bachelor party to get to in a few hours."

"I hope you aren't planning on drinking yourself into a stupor."

He looked insulted. "Me? I've never drunk myself into more than half a stupor, and that was a long time ago. Don't worry about me—I'm the guy in charge of the party. It's my job to make sure Artie is able to make it to the wedding tomorrow."

He picked up his packed case, but didn't move immediately. His eyes burned into hers for a few seconds and then he turned away and walked out of the house. Kendall stood in the doorway and watched him toss the case into the car and gun the engine. Then she shut the door. She didn't want to watch him leave.

But she heard him. The sound of the engine faded away and the house was left in silence. Not so much as the ticking of a clock disturbed the serenity.

Then a high-pitched whistle creased the air and Harpo flew from his perch to land on the back of the sofa where he eyed her with his head cocked to one side.

"Well, Harpo, what do you usually do for fun on a Friday night?"

Harpo let out a wolf whistle.

By seven-thirty that evening Kendall had investigated both Jared's library and record collection, made herself dinner, eaten and cleaned up, watched the news on television and was now watching a game show.

"What is Machu Picchu," she blurted out at the TV screen. "Idiot," she said when the contestant got it wrong.

"Pick Shakespeare for four hundred," she said to the television people.

They picked mathematics. Kendall groaned. The telephone rang.

She turned the television sound off and reached out and picked up the receiver. "Hello?"

There was a pause, then, "Is Jared there?"

Kendall scowled. The voice was very feminine and sounded very attractive. "No, I'm sorry, he isn't. Can I take a message?"

"That depends. Who are you?"

"My name is Kendall Arden," she said politely. "And who are you?"

"I'm Cynthia Lindstrom. And I didn't mean who are you, I meant what are you to Jared?"

Cynthia sounded a teensy-weensy bit irritated. And if Cynthia was a little detail that Jared failed to mention, Kendall thought that she may just plot a murder this weekend.

"Actually, Ms. Lindstrom, I was just thinking the same thing. What are you to Jared?"

Kendall was sure she could hear the woman sputtering. "Never mind. Just tell him I called."

"Oh, I will."

Hanging up, Kendall turned and looked at Harpo. "It's a pity you can't talk, Harpo, because I really want to know what that woman is to Jared. Or was. In any case, if that's his normal taste in women, I think I'm insulted."

What she didn't say to Harpo was that just the thought of Jared's seeing that woman, or any other woman, caused her heart to clench painfully. Knowing she had absolutely no right to feel that way didn't help in the least. In fact, it only made her feel worse.

Just as she reached out to turn the television volume back up, the telephone rang again.

"If that's another of his women, I'm outta here. Hello?"

"What did I do?"

"Oh, hi, Chloe. Nothing. I just got a call from a real witch of a woman who was looking for Jared and seemed quite disturbed to hear my voice."

Chloe chuckled. "I suppose you just told her you were a house-and bird-sitting colleague?"

"No, I'm afraid I forgot to mention that."

This time they both laughed.

"I just thought I'd give you a call and see how you were doing."

"I'm fine, Chloe. Just a little restless. And talking to Cynthia didn't help."

"I doubt if you did much for Cynthia's night, either."

"Chloe, what if he's been going out with Cynthia all along?" Kendall asked.

"What if he has? Would that bother you?"

Yes, of course it would! she felt like shouting. Instead she kept her voice even. "I don't see why it should. It isn't like we're close or anything. I'm just curious, that's all. That woman didn't sound like Jared's type, that's all."

"And what type *is* Jared's type?"

Hearing the smugness in Chloe's voice, Kendall snapped, "I have no idea, but it isn't Cynthia Lindstrom."

Chloe just laughed. "Honestly, Kendall, just listen to yourself. Maybe you'd learn something."

Harpo jumped from one branch to another and tilted his head sideways to eye Kendall. She picked up one of the nuts she'd shelled earlier and gave it to him. "Like what?" she asked Chloe warily.

"Like why it is that you're suddenly jealous of a woman you've never seen—"

"I am not!"

"—and why you think you know what type of woman a man you say *you* won't go out with *should* go out with."

Kendall paused to sort out what her friend had just said. Then she scowled. "Chloe, have you been drinking?"

Laughter tripped over the telephone wires. "No, but maybe you should get a glass of wine, put on some jazz and just mellow out, Kendall. I'm sure it'll all become clear if you think about it awhile."

"I don't think I want it all to become clear," Kendall griped.

"Fighting your feelings won't make them go away," Chloe said gently.

Kendall was becoming increasingly aware of that. The knowledge made her uncomfortable. "That may be true, Chloe, but I have no choice but to at least ignore them. Even if I didn't, there's no way we could be together."

"Why not? Because of your stupid rule?"

"Yes, partially. And it isn't stupid. Beyond that, though, I'm probably ruining his project."

After briefly but succinctly describing her dreams and the fact that she couldn't bring herself to tell them to Jared, Kendall fell silent, wondering if somehow Chloe might come up with a solution she hadn't thought of.

"Wow," her roommate finally said. "That *is* a problem. Why didn't you tell me before?"

"I don't know, Chloe. What good would it have done? Besides, you have enough to worry about with your own project and Brice and your teaching."

"I always have time for my friends, Kendall. Especially you. And I wish I could tell you what to do now, but I can't. You have to do what you think is right."

Kendall nodded at Harpo. "I know. But I can't bring myself to tell him. Those dreams reveal too much, Chloe, and I'd feel totally humiliated if he knew about them. Can you imagine having to work with a man all the time who knows that you've had erotic dreams about him? Besides, he'd hate me for holding back information from his project. What if he kicked me off his project and refused to participate in mine?"

"Do you really think Jared would do that?"

Kendall knew he wouldn't. "Well, no. But I'm not going to risk finding out at this point."

"I can't say you're wrong to be cautious, but there should be a way for all of this to work."

"If you can figure it out, Chloe, let me know."

"I will" came the determined reply.

"And thanks for calling. I needed to have this conversation."

"No problem. I'll call again tomorrow, just to check your boredom level."

After hanging up, Kendall turned up the sound for the finale of the show, but didn't pay much attention. Not feeling like watching it anymore, she turned the TV set off. Harpo was eyeing the nuts again, and Kendall fed him one.

"What am I to do, Harpo? If I tell him the truth he'll probably hate me. But if I don't, I'll hate myself. I don't know why I have to have those stupid dreams about him all the time, anyway," she grumbled.

Actually Kendall was afraid that she was beginning to know why, but she didn't want to think about that, either. One thing she did know—right now she could handle hating herself better than the prospect of Jared's hating her.

She just couldn't risk it, Kendall decided. "I'll have to ignore what I feel for him," she said aloud. "And hope that he doesn't push it anymore." Harpo cocked his head, but Kendall wondered if he was really listening or just begging for more nuts. "I'm going crazy and you want nuts. Here." She handed him another one. He whistled at her.

"You lech. Who taught you that? Never mind. It had to be Jared. And wouldn't that go over great among the gossip mongers at school? Kendall loves Jared," she said in the singsong voice children use to tease each other. "No, forget I said that. I'm really not in love. It's only a crush or chemistry or something. I don't date coworkers and I certainly don't fall in love with them. Not that it isn't possible that I could fall in love with him—in which case everything would be even worse...."

Her wandering thoughts made her shudder and she stopped talking. The whole thing spelled disaster. Getting up, she retrieved her bag and opened it, pulling out the evaluations she'd brought to work on this weekend.

As she sat down under the watchful gaze of Harpo, Kendall forced all thoughts of Jared from her mind. She had a project to finish and nothing—not even her growing feelings for the man—were going to get in her way. She wanted to win that grant, and the only thing that dulled her enthusiasm were her own constant reminders to herself that she wasn't playing fair by holding out on Jared.

Sunday afternoon found Kendall in the same place she'd been Friday night: studying her surveys and making notes for her project. She'd slept on the sofa in the living room both nights, not wanting to torture herself by sleeping in Jared's bed.

Harpo had been a good bird, although his sudden bursts of whistling or screeching still made her jump. Fortunately he'd been quiet at night.

Now he let out a screech and several whistles. Kendall just ignored him until she heard gravel crunching under tires outside. Harpo whistled again and Kendall felt a lot of fluttery sensations, but was determined to control them.

She got up and straightened her sweater, pausing to shove her feet into her loafers before she went to the door. She pulled it open just as Jared reached the small front porch. His gaze was as penetrating as ever, and Kendall was forced to look away.

"Welcome home. How was the wedding?"

He came in and dropped his suitcase in the hall and shut the door. "It was a bash, but for some reason, not as much fun as I thought it would be. I was thinking too much about...uh...my project."

"Well, that's understandable," Kendall said evenly. She'd almost let herself hope he was going to say he was thinking about her, but then she reminded herself that she wasn't going to give in to her emotions.

"How was it here?" he asked.

"Oh, fine. I did some work on my project and Harpo whistled at me all weekend. He's a very fresh bird."

Jared cleared his throat. "Is he?"

Walking over to the tree where the cockatoo lived, Jared held out his hand and Harpo climbed on. Then he was transferred onto Jared's shoulder, where he danced a little, then sat still. His dark eyes still ogled Kendall, though.

"Have you been bothering Kendall?"

"Kendall," Harpo squawked.

Jared's jaw dropped, and Kendall's eyebrows shot up. "I thought you said he couldn't talk."

"Actually I said he *didn't* talk. He never has before now. Only whistles and screeches. Kendall," he said to the bird.

"Kendall," Harpo repeated clearly. "Kendall's a sexy number."

To say the silence was awkward was an understatement. Then Jared cleared his throat again and looked from Harpo to Kendall. "Uh, I know that sounds bad... Well, not bad, but sexist maybe, and I can explain."

Kendall didn't need an explanation. Jared had called her a sexy number in front of Harpo, and now the bird was repeating it. The fact that Jared found her sexy was flattering, but she hardly registered it.

No, what caused Kendall's face to pale was a simple progression of ideas. Jared had said something and Harpo later repeated it. It was cute and essentially harmless. But she had also said things to Harpo, thinking he couldn't talk. And those things could prove disastrous to Kendall Arden. At the top of the list were the words *Kendall loves Jared*. Why hadn't she kept her mouth shut? She rationalized that Harpo probably wouldn't remember such a little phrase, anyway.

"Kendall? You aren't offended, are you?"

She blinked and his face came into focus. It was odd, but Jared looked a little red around the neck. Ordinarily Kendall would have found the fact that he was embarrassed by his bird endearing, but she was too distressed.

"No, I'm not offended." It was amazing how normal her voice sounded, she thought. Especially considering that her world could come crashing down around her at any minute. "Er, he has to hear something a lot to repeat it, doesn't he?"

"Actually, no. I only said that once to him—really. Well, maybe twice. But that's all."

Kendall smiled weakly and said, "I guess he's just a late bloomer, then, huh?"

If the bird opened his beak and ratted on her, she would just tell Jared it was a joke. Because it was a joke…wasn't it?

"Would you like me to take you home, or would you like to stay for dinner? I have some steaks in the freezer."

Kendall shook her head. "I don't think so. I appreciate the offer, but I really should be getting back. I have laundry and shopping to do."

Lame excuses, she knew, considering that she had the whole of the next week to do chores and errands, but Jared didn't call her on it. He just nodded and put Harpo back in his tree.

Jared then picked up her bag and headed for the door. Kendall gathered the papers she'd been working on and turned to follow him.

The last thing she heard as she left Jared's house was Harpo. "Kendall is a sexy number," he squawked.

Chapter Seven

Jared felt as though he'd missed the second act of a play. He'd seen the first and was now back for the third, but no one would tell him what had transpired during the second.

He'd left town knowing that he and Kendall needed to talk about what was happening between them. He knew that Kendall probably had good reasons for wanting to stick to her rule. But Jared had discovered something himself—which was that he wanted to see more of Kendall Arden. A lot more.

That had been a revelation to him. He had spent the whole weekend in Baltimore wondering what Kendall was doing and thinking that he would be having a better time if she were there.

He had even dreamed about her. Twice. The first dream hadn't surprised him. It had been sexual and not too unlike the waking fantasies involving Kendall he'd recently caught himself indulging in. No, that dream hadn't really been unexpected, titillating though it was.

The dream that still had him wondering was one where they had just been strolling along some sort of path in a park or wooded area. They were holding hands and just walking. The path changed to a beach, then to a sidewalk. Then they had to go up several hills. But they never stopped holding hands and they never spoke.

Looking over the entry now in his journal, Jared frowned. They hadn't spoken aloud, but he had known what Kendall was thinking. And she had known what he was thinking. And feeling. It was the most intriguing dream he'd ever had, and as a psychologist, he knew that there were any number of interpretations he could hang on it, but he chose not to interpret it all—at least not yet. At present he was more concerned with the fact that he thought about Kendall so much while he was awake.

That had never happened to him before, and he wasn't sure he liked it. To suspect that he was really beginning to care for Kendall—or any woman—that much made him uncomfortable. Women were nice to have around, to touch and kiss and make love with, but eventually they interfered with his life. They became jealous of his dedication to his work and they inevitably were hurt by the fact that he loved his work more than them.

Would Kendall be the same? Somehow Jared couldn't fit Kendall into the mold that other women in his life had fit. For one thing, she didn't fall into his arms like most women. Jared wasn't really used to having to pursue the attentions of a woman. He was finding it both stimulating and frustrating. And confusing.

With any other woman, he would have accepted her rejection with a smile and forgotten it. He found himself unable or unwilling to do that with Kendall. He'd determined that when he returned home from the wedding they could talk and come to some conclusions. Yet the moment he'd stepped back into his house, he'd known something was wrong.

Kendall had seemed a little quiet, though otherwise calm, when he'd first come in. Then, after Harpo's sudden vocalization, she'd become tense and preoccupied. Certain she'd been insulted by the fact that Harpo had called her a sexy number, he'd been surprised when Kendall had just shrugged it off. He'd driven her home and hadn't gotten three complete sentences out of her the whole time.

Then, as she'd climbed out of the car, she'd turned back and, looking straight at his collar button, said, "Oh, I almost forgot. Cynthia Lindstrom called while you were away. She didn't leave a message."

With that she darted away and up the steps to her front door. Jared had been left sitting in the car and staring after her. Cynthia had called? What had she said to Kendall? Was that why Kendall was acting so strangely?

Monday evening he still hadn't been able to come up with any satisfactory answers. He decided to call Cynthia, more out of curiosity than a desire to talk with her. They hadn't dated in three or four months and had parted without animosity—at least on his part.

Picking up the telephone, he opened his address book and punched out Cynthia's number.

"Jared, how wonderful to hear from you."

"Cynthia, I got a message that you called."

A pause, then a deep sigh. "Yes. I don't know who that person is to you, but she was very rude to me. I didn't know you were living with someone, Jared. After all, we'd been going out so recently..."

Jared smiled at Cynthia's transparency. "She isn't living with me, Cyn. She was only house-sitting. I was in Baltimore for my cousin's wedding."

"Oh, how wonderful," Cynthia gushed. "I love weddings."

He didn't doubt that. "I'm sorry I didn't return your call earlier, but I've been rather busy."

"With work, I suppose," she said resignedly.

"That's right."

"Well, anyway, I was just calling to see if you might escort me to a charity ball next Friday night. It'll be a lot of fun. It's going to be held at my brother's country club near Aberdeen. There'll be sailing..."

Jared couldn't muster even one iota of interest in seeing Cynthia again—even though the prospect of night sailing was being dangled before him like a carrot. "I'm sure it would be a great time, Cyn, but I can't. I'm working nights on my project."

Cynthia sighed dramatically. "Jared, I know your work is the most important thing in your life, but really, you're becoming positively dull. And forgive me for not being deep enough to understand, but your work can't love you or keep your bed warm."

When Jared didn't say anything, Cynthia laughed. "Oh, I don't know why I'm bothering. Love isn't something you understand, is it, Jared? I mean love for a woman. You love your family and God knows you love your work, but until you fall in love, if you ever do, you'll never understand what I'm talking about."

"I guess you're right, Cyn."

"For some reason, being right doesn't do much for my feminine ego. Well, I have to go, Jared. I hope you do find someone. She'll have to be really special, though, to compete with your work."

"Yes, I suppose she will," he said quietly before saying goodbye. He gazed at his hand resting on the receiver for several seconds before noticing his watch.

It was time he walked over to get Kendall. He closed his dream journal and shoved it into a row of books on his shelf behind the desk. He collected his coat and headed up the steps to the side door. When he opened it, he heard a startled gasp. Kendall was standing there with her fist raised.

"What did I do now?" he asked.

Her big round eyes blinked, then she looked away. "Nothing. I was just about to knock."

"I thought I told you I didn't like your walking around by yourself at night."

He knew he was sounding bossy, but there were too many things that could happen to women alone, and the thought of any of them happening to Kendall worried him more than he liked to admit.

"It's only three blocks," Kendall said, as though that made everything all right.

"I suppose that muggers and rapists all have a rule about not attacking people within three blocks of their destinations."

Finally, he thought, she was looking at him. Her expression was hard to read in the shadows, but Jared had the impression she was a little indignant from the way her slender body tensed.

"I've managed to take care of myself for twenty-five years," she contended. "And I don't like the idea of you, or anyone, thinking they need to look out for me. I've taken self-defense courses and I have Mace."

Jared thought it was just as well it was fairly dark, because he was sure Kendall would be incensed at the way he'd just rolled his eyes. "Well, I guess that's something," he muttered as he held the door open for her and followed her down to the lab.

She took off her coat and hung it up, shifting her ever-present backpack onto her shoulder and crossing her arms over her chest before she turned to face him.

It was a blatant defense stance and Jared knew that Kendall understood what she was doing. She was telling him to back off. There were only two problems with that. One was that he wanted to know why and the other was that he didn't want to back off.

"Where's Larry?"

"I think I told you before that he was taking a four-day weekend. He'll be back tomorrow. Do you miss him?"

She shrugged. "Not really, I just forgot you'd told me that."

Setting his jaw, Jared decided that Kendall could be stubborn if she wanted, but he could be just as persistent. "Why don't you tell me what's wrong?"

She swallowed noticeably and avoided eye contact. "Nothing's wrong."

"Then why are you so nervous?"

"I'm not nervous," she declared, but her voice wavered.

"Do I make you nervous, Kendall?"

He wasn't sure if he liked the thought or not. But it had definite possibilities.

"No, you don't. I wanted to ask you if we could start working on my project this week. I had Chloe go through the training process already. Once you do it, we can all go through the evaluations and see if my theory has any validity."

He sighed at her evasion of his question, but didn't push her anymore. Jared knew she had her reasons for not wanting to get involved, but he was discovering that he had equally good reasons for wanting to. And at the top of his list was that he wanted Kendall, and from what she'd shown him when he'd kissed her, she wanted him. But even more than wanting her body, he wanted her mind and her sense of humor and her heart. But he knew that she would run if he told her that, so he just smiled and said, "Name the time."

Smoky-gray eyes collided with his and Jared saw that she was more than surprised. She looked suspicious and a little fearful. "What do you mean?"

"I mean that I'm ready to work on your project. You've been working on mine and doing a great job. Now it's time for me to work on yours."

Her eyes closed, and when she opened them, she was looking at his collar button again. "Jared, I...that is...thanks. Can we start tomorrow morning, before you leave to go home?"

"Sure," he said after a moment. Why had she suddenly looked so morose? Jared was certain she'd been about to tell him something. Curious, he said softly, "Kendall, what's troubling you? It's more than your project, isn't it? I hope it isn't me."

Her eyes darted to his and then away. "I guess it is, in a way. You haven't made things very easy for me, Jared."

"Why?" he asked. "Because of this rule of yours?" When she just nodded, he pressed her. "Why do you feel so strongly about it?"

For a moment he thought she was going to refuse to answer him. Then her shoulders shifted and she let her pack slide down her arm. She dropped it into a chair and went over to fiddle with one of the sleep-monitoring instruments.

"My rule wasn't made until this past year. I'd never had a reason for it before, since it was my first real job. I had just gotten my doctorate and had been hired at a small college in Ohio. It was kind of far from my family—I'm originally from Newport News in Virginia—but it was a good opportunity and I liked the college.''

"I take it something happened to change that."

Kendall laughed bitterly. "Just before Christmas, one of the other psych professors asked me out. There were only six of us in the department. Anyway, he was attractive, and I was still trying to make friends and get to know people. I didn't see the harm."

"So you went out with him."

"Yes. And we had a good time. I enjoyed the party we went to and all. After that, he asked me out again, and again."

Jared didn't like where this conversation seemed to be headed. But since he'd started it, he pressed on. "And you fell in love with him?"

Her eyes swung up to meet his. "Oh, no. He was nice and all, but to be honest, Joel didn't, uh, well...that is, he kissed me a few times, but I didn't really like it very much." She suddenly frowned and looked away. "I never seemed to like kissing very much. I used to think I was frigid."

Jared couldn't help the laugh that escaped him. Kendall blushed several becoming shades of red and scowled at him. "I'm sorry, Kendall. But I find that amusing. Because you haven't given me the impression of being frigid at all. I also got the feeling that you enjoyed kissing...me."

Her cheeks got redder. "I've changed, I guess. Anyway," she hurried on, "I didn't fall in love with him. But he, apparently, had become enamored enough of me to ask me to marry him."

Jared's pleasure at Kendall's admission that she liked kissing him and not other men was promptly overshadowed by something he was afraid was very like jealousy. "I take it you turned him down?"

"Yes. But Joel didn't take rejection very well. He decided that I simply needed convincing. So he sent me flowers and candy every day. He called me every night. He told the other people we worked with that he would get me to say yes and that I was just playing hard to get."

"What did they think?"

"They thought it was cute for a couple of weeks. Then it got to be a nuisance. He interrupted their work and wasn't doing his own job properly."

Jared shook his head. "Why didn't the department head have a word with him?"

Kendall stopped her restless wandering and sat down. "He did. That's when Joel got mean. He accused me of leading him on and them dumping him. He stopped sending all the flowers and calling me. But he also refused to talk to me unless he had to, and then he was rude and sarcastic. After a couple of months, my nerves were shot and my work was suffering. I've never been so unhappy in my life. It was then that I decided to get another job and try to start over."

"And so you made a rule never to date someone you worked with."

"That's right. It was just too traumatic, and I don't want to have to go through something like that again. I really like CSU and want to stay here. I hope you understand now why I've put you off. Under other circumstances, it might have been different."

Not liking the implication in her words, Jared's jaw tensed. "I hope you don't think I would do something like that jerk did?"

Her eyes met his calmly now. "No, I don't think you would. But when human emotions are involved, things happen that wouldn't normally. And I'm not sophisticated enough to be able to have an affair with someone I work with and then break it off and not feel awkward around that person. So I made my rule. It may not be an ideal solution, but it's the only one I have."

As he looked down at her pinched features, Jared felt frustrated. He wanted to tell her that it would be different with them, but he couldn't. He also didn't relish the fact that she was automatically assuming that if they started a relationship, it wouldn't last. His track record with women wouldn't make a very convincing argument on that front. As much as he resisted the idea, maybe she was right.

"I can't say I like it," he finally said, "but I respect it. And I can't say that I'll stop wanting you, Kendall, because it isn't that easy. But I won't press you into anything you don't want. I still want to be friends, if that's possible, because I do like you, and you're a very special person."

Kendall just smiled shakily at him through watery eyes. Jared didn't totally believe everything he'd just said, or even thought, but if it helped Kendall relax a little and smile again, then it was worth it.

Kendall hadn't thought that having a conversation could be so exhausting. But as she picked up her backpack and entered the wildflower bedroom, she had to admit that telling Jared about Joel had been draining. The only other person she'd ever told had been Chloe. Joel wasn't a subject she liked to talk about.

And now Jared knew. She'd wondered while telling him if he would think she'd been a fool for the way she'd handled Joel, but Jared hadn't seemed to think less of her for any of her actions.

And she hadn't meant to tell him that Joel's kisses had left her cold or that most men's kisses had left her cold. And she really had wondered about her own ability to respond normally—that is, she'd wondered until Jared had kissed her. Her response to him had surprised her and confused her. She longed for more, but knew that it couldn't be.

Because as depressing as the idea was, Kendall knew that if she let herself get involved with Jared she would be devastated by losing him. And she didn't see how it could end any other way. While Jared seemed to feel desire for her, he hadn't indicated that he was interested in more than a physical relationship. And Kendall knew she would want so much more from him.

Dragging herself into the bathroom, she prepared for bed and slipped into a huge T-shirt with the CSU logo on it. It came down to her knees and the sleeves hung down to her elbows, so she felt it was modest enough.

Looking at herself in the bathroom mirror, she remembered the sound of Harpo's squawky voice telling her she was a sexy number. Then her smile faded and anxiety took over. Harpo had obviously repeated what he'd heard Jared saying, and while it was flattering to know that Jared thought she was sexy, it was nerve-racking to know that the pink bird could decide to repeat something she'd said in his presence, as well.

It was hard enough to resist Jared when he knew she was attracted to him, but if he thought that she had actually been foolish enough to fall in love with him . . . Kendall gulped. She wouldn't think about it—worrying about it wouldn't do any good, anyway.

Turning off the light, she made her way back into the bedroom, dragging her backpack with her. One thing she had looked forward to after her student years were over was being able to discard her backpack. And now she was lugging the thing around again.

Climbing into bed, she arranged the pillows the way she liked them and then pulled out her notes on the final phase of her project. Jared had actually seemed interested in starting his part. Of course, then he'd made her feel awful by complimenting her work on *his* project. Every day that went by made her feel worse for deceiving him about those stupid dreams.

After an hour, she decided she might as well try to get to sleep, since she didn't seem to be able to concentrate, anyway. She hadn't slept very well the night before and now hoped she wouldn't lie awake half the night again.

She pulled the clipboard from the nightstand and filled in what she'd eaten and her emotional state during the day. She didn't fudge it, either, since she knew that Jared was aware she'd been upset and nervous most of the day.

She didn't remember falling asleep, but she knew she was dreaming when she saw herself being pulled in different directions by Jared and her research notes, which had grown hands. When her notes then began trying to eat her, and succeeding, she awoke with a start.

"Uh . . . I just dreamed that I was being attacked by my project, which had hands and then a mouth. It was huge, bigger than me, but I couldn't control it and it ate me."

Mostly that was true, but Kendall refused to admit that Jared had been in her dream. She had recorded all of the dreams that he'd been in, and she did intend to give her notes to him once they'd completed their work. It would be too difficult to let him know before then.

Looking at her illuminated watch, she saw that it was two in the morning. Sighing deeply, she turned on her side and tried to go back to sleep.

Jared was walking toward her, his shoulders slumped. Kendall looked up at him. "What's wrong?"

"My project's a bust. If you didn't want to be in my project, why didn't you just quit? Why did you have to lie and ruin the whole thing for me?"

She felt a tap on her shoulder. Turning, she saw Dr. Grady shaking his head. "Dr. Arden, I'm disappointed. You know, of course, you've been disqualified from the grant competition. This is highly unethical. Shame on you."

Dr. Grady was walking away. "Wait," Kendall called. "I didn't mean to hurt his project."

Suddenly her parents were there. "We're so disappointed, Kendall," her mother was saying. "We told you that lying is wrong. And now look what you've done."

Then they walked away.

"Wait, I'm sorry, I won't do it again."

Jared grabbed her arms then and pulled her close to him. "I cared for you. I even helped you with your stupid astrology project, and then you lied to me? Why?"

"I'm sorry. I was afraid to tell you I was dreaming about you. I was afraid you'd laugh at me."

"I wouldn't do that. I'm a scientist."

"I know," she said, trying to pull away, but his arms held her fast. "But I couldn't let you know I was dreaming of you like that, thinking of you like that."

"Why not? They were just dreams. You didn't really mean them, did you? Did you?"

She was shaking her head. "No...I mean, yes...I don't know. Please don't hate me, Jared."

"Why shouldn't I? You ruined my work. I'll never get that grant now, and it's your fault."

"I'm sorry."

"It's too late for regrets, Kendall."

"But it can't be. Jared... I love you!"

Holding her in a vice grip, he laughed down at her as she struggled against him. "Love? You don't know what the word means. You don't love someone and lie to them. I hate you."

"No!"

She cried out and tried to get away, but couldn't. She felt trapped and pushed against him, finally pulling violently away. But once he released her, Kendall suddenly felt herself falling and crashing.

"Kendall? Are you all right?"

Lying on the floor, the sheets twisted around her legs, Kendall let out a sigh of frustration and dropped her head into her hands. Her heart was beating furiously and she was perspiring.

"Kendall?"

The intercom no longer had its usual static, Kendall thought. Then when she felt a hand touch her shoulder, she nearly leapt out of her skin. "Good Lord, Jared, you scared me to death."

"You should have answered me. Are you all right?"

"I'm fine," she said, struggling to untangle her legs. "Just incredibly embarrassed."

"Well, don't be." He sounded relieved. Grasping her hand, he pulled her to her feet and tossed the covers back onto the bed.

Kendall pushed her hair out of her eyes and looked warily at Jared, who was gazing calmly at her. Except for the suppressed laughter she could see dancing in his dark eyes, Kendall might have thought he was serious. But he wasn't. He was laughing at her.

"It's nice of you to be so concerned, Jared," Kendall said without a trace of sarcasm. She turned away from him slightly and with her hands felt the bed behind her. "I really am all right, in spite of my inglorious fall."

"I had to make sure you were in one piece. It wasn't easy watching you fall out of bed like that, but that's part of the— Oof!"

He hadn't seen the pillow coming, and after striking once, Kendall pulled back to do it again. She would have hit him on the head, but he straightened and she only managed a glancing blow off his shoulder.

"That's for being so concerned on the outside while laughing on the inside."

Jared reached for the pillow, but Kendall dodged him by scrambling over the bed. "What do you mean? I wasn't laughing at you!"

"Your mouth wasn't laughing, but your eyes were."

Standing on the opposite side of the bed, Kendall could still feel the heat radiating from Jared's body. When he'd helped her up, it had been all she could do to keep from pressing closer instead of backing away. Now he stood smiling at her with a gleam in his eye.

"So, you think you can read my thoughts in my eyes, Kendall? What am I thinking right now?"

Kendall hugged her pillow to her chest and looked at him. She saw that he was planning something. Retaliation, most likely. Suddenly she started to laugh.

In one fluid motion, he grabbed another pillow and sent it sailing at her.

Ducking easily, Kendall looked over her shoulder to see where it landed against the wall. "Your aim isn't so great, is—"

She let out a yelp when she realized he had thrown the pillow only as a diversion. He'd then climbed over the bed and grabbed the pillow that she held against her. Her natural instinct was to hold on, but Jared had tugged harder and she fell toward him with a startled yelp.

Her body hit the bed beside him and he pulled the pillow from her surprised hands and held it above her. Kendall automatically shut her eyes. But instead of a pillow hitting her, she felt Jared's lips touching hers.

She was too startled to do more than react with her instincts. So she kissed him back. It was when she felt his hands burning her skin through the thin material of her T-shirt that she realized where they were and what they were doing.

Kendall pushed at his shoulder and Jared kissed her once more before pulling away a few inches. She had to blink her eyes a few times to focus. "This wasn't what we agreed upon," she whispered raggedly.

Jared smiled ruefully down at her. "Maybe not. But I think we need a new agreement. Because any agreement that doesn't include kissing is a bad agreement."

Then his head lowered again and Kendall's eyes drifted shut in a haze of pleasure. But it was only a few moments before Jared lifted his head again and sighed. "As much as I would rather kiss you, I need to find out how much of that dream you were having you remember."

The mention of her dream cleared away the fog in Kendall's brain. She rolled away, cursing herself for her weakness where Jared was concerned. "All I remember is that Dr. Grady was telling me that I'd disappointed him and that I'd lost the grant competition."

Jared sighed. "You don't ever seem to dream about anything but your project."

Kendall refrained from telling him that he figured in her dreams as much or more than her project. "Well, it's been on my mind a lot. And it's not all I ever dream about. Last night I dreamed that I was on a treasure hunt—sort of like Indiana Jones. But for some reason, when I'm here, my work shows up more often."

Contemplating this, Jared rose from the bed and paced for a few moments. Then he stopped and looked at her. "Maybe it's because you're always working on it right before you go to sleep. I think it's time for you to move on to the next phase of the experiment."

Kendall wasn't sure she wanted to hear what that was. "Which is?"

"Control. We'll start off just by giving you something else to read before you sleep. If that works, we'll go on to verbal suggestions."

With that, he started for the door. Just before reaching it, he wheeled around suddenly, catching Kendall as her eyes were moving appreciatively over his taut backside. "You lech," he laughed as she hid her red face in the pillow. "What do you want for breakfast?"

"Nothing," she mumbled into the pillow.

"What was that? Scrambled eggs, sausage and orange juice? Be right back."

Kendall jerked her head up and began to protest, but Jared was gone. She sighed and beat her head against the pillow. As a way to start off her resolution to keep her relationship with Jared platonic, this morning was a disaster.

Sighing, she pulled a piece of paper from her pack and wrote down all the details of the dream that she could remember—distasteful as they were.

As she wrote, she saw the words, but didn't think about them until they were there on the paper. She'd told Jared in her dream that she loved him. She didn't really, though, did she? She looked again at what she'd written. He was right, even if he'd said it in a dream. You didn't lie to someone you loved. Gritting her teeth and shaking her head, she refused to think about that dream. But she didn't really want to think about her project, either.

Jared was right about that. She was dreaming about her project too much. Maybe her mind was trying to tell her something. She still had almost a month before the work was due to be delivered to the grant committee. And she was ahead of schedule.

"Back off a little, Kendall," she told herself. It was spring break, she thought as she made her way to the bathroom. Maybe she would take a few days and do a little pleasure reading. Go for a long walk around the deserted campus. Maybe she'd even see if Chloe would like to take in a movie. Kendall couldn't remember the last time she'd seen a movie.

From the bathroom, Kendall heard Jared return. "Come on and eat before it gets cold," he called.

Kendall shrugged. Her short hair was still wet, but would probably dry on its own while she ate. She paused when she remembered that she hadn't put on any cosmetics yet. Then she set her chin and continued forward. Maybe seeing her in her natural state would give Jared pause.

It didn't appear, though, to give him pause, or anything else. He simply smiled at her when she walked in, and finished laying out the food. Kendall sat down and reached for a piece of sausage.

"So, what are you planning to do with your spring break?" he asked.

She swallowed and looked at him. "I'm going to train you on your part of my project, and after doing that I'm going to rest. All these dreams I've been having are probably pointing out the fact that I need a break. So I'm going to relax for a few days and read a book that isn't academic, take a few leisurely strolls, maybe go to the movies."

"That sounds like a good idea. Stress does often manifest itself in repetitive dreams. What are you thinking of reading?"

"I have no idea. But it won't be on any recommended reading list. What are you going to do?"

Jared sipped his coffee and smiled again. "I'll be here, listening to dreams. Of course, I'd rather be sailing. Maybe I'll do that over the weekend."

Kendall's eyes lit up. "You sail?"

He nodded. "When I can. I have a twenty-five-foot sloop at a marina near Havre de Grace. She's been sitting there all winter. I was thinking that I might get down there one day soon and take her out into the bay."

Kendall was filled with a longing she hadn't felt in ages. She imagined that Chesapeake Bay in early spring would be wonderful. The crowds wouldn't be out yet, and the wind would be gusty enough to make for a challenging sail.

"I love to sail, but I haven't been sailing in more than two years," she said.

Jared, a cup of coffee at his lips, sputtered suddenly, but when Kendall looked curiously at him, he just shook his head. "I guess it went down the wrong way. Uh, so you're a sailor, too?"

She laughed. "After a fashion. My father has a sailboat and we used to go as a family once or twice a month. How my parents managed all of us is still a mystery to me. From a distance the boat probably looked like it was swarming with orange ants because of our life jackets."

"There was a swarm of you?"

"Well, five kids and my parents. We took the dog once, but he didn't turn out to be such a great seaman. After that, my dad banned him from future sails."

"Were you the oldest?"

Kendall laughed. "Yes. The textbook overachiever and take-charge type. I'm a case study for proponents of birth-order studies." Casting an assessing gaze at Jared, she said, "You're an only child, aren't you?"

He grinned and nodded. "Too much time spent alone either makes a master criminal or a scholar."

"How about a bank robber with really good grades?" Kendall suggested.

Jared laughed and then leaned forward, his forearms resting on the desk. "Kendall, you are amazing. Did you know that?"

"Yes, I did," she said immodestly. "But it's nice to hear someone else agree with me once in a while."

He laughed with her. "Well, I do."

Kendall shook her head at their silly conversation. And as much as she enjoyed just sitting and talking with him, she really did have to get him trained in her theory so that he could do the evaluations with her and Chloe.

"I know you're not really interested, but can we get on to your part in my project now? It really shouldn't take all that long, since you've already read my notes and all."

Jared's eyebrows rose. "What makes you think I'm not interested?"

"I know you're not," Kendall said. "If I hadn't come begging, you wouldn't have wanted anything to do with the subject. I do appreciate the fact that you've been as open-minded as you have been, though."

"You're welcome," Jared said sardonically. "And since I've been reading your theory, I've decided that perhaps I was too quick to judge. It really is interesting."

Kendall was pleased, but not totally convinced of his sincerity. "Thanks, but let's see how you feel after going through it all with me."

They cleared off his desk and Kendall got her materials from her backpack. She explained the common and associated traits of each zodiac sign and Jared nodded. "Right. I got that from your notes."

"What I'm doing is taking the evaluations people have filled out and matching the traits people give themselves and then matching them to the appropriate sign. There's a four percent margin of error figured for people who may not describe themselves honestly. Anyway, once you, Chloe and I all go through the surveys and evaluate them, I'll be able to calculate whether or not my theory has any merit. If you two can successfully match traits to signs, then other people could as well. This project is really only the beginning of a much bigger study. But it's an important hurdle."

"Then let's get started!"

Two hours later, Jared stood and stretched. "I believe that my mind has had enough."

"That's okay," Kendall allowed, "since we're finished, anyway. Now all you have to do is take all this home and go over it a few times on your own. Then you'll be ready to begin the evaluation stage."

"I think I want to make a test run."

"What do you mean?"

His eyes twinkled mischievously. "I am ready to guess your sign."

"It shouldn't be a matter of guessing, Jared," Kendall began, but he held up a hand.

"I'm ready to evaluate you, then." He cleared his throat. "I think you are an Aquarius. The water bearer.

An air sign. Just like me. That means we're mental creatures—original thinkers. Aquarius is a fixed sign, which means you like to establish yourself and not move, or be moved, against your will. You're honorable, honest and trustworthy.

"As an Aquarius, you're progressive and broad-minded. You're also unselfish, and humanitarian instincts run deep in your character. Your concern for people probably influenced your decision to study psychology. You're good at controlling your temper, but your greatest fault is procrastination.

"You're stubborn, and likely to set your own rules to live by if the ones around you don't suit you." Kendall opened her mouth, but Jared held up a hand to silence her. "Aquarian women sometimes seem cool and aloof while at the same time radiating sexual warmth and charm. As far as romance is concerned, Aquarians are most suited to Geminis, Leos and...Librans. And I didn't make that up."

Kendall just stared at him. "Did you really interpret me and my traits, or did you sneak a peak at my driver's license?"

Jared burst into laughter. "I was right!"

"Yes, you were. I was born January thirtieth. And I'm glad to see that you were interested enough in my research to go and look up some things on your own. As for your last, er, findings, I should have known that you'd find those traits most interesting. But beyond that, your ability to evaluate traits just reiterates that my theory is valid and deserves to be looked at and considered with respect. You did a great job," she said quietly. "But I really should be going now. I have to check in at the post office for additional surveys that might have come in."

His remarks about her honesty and loyalty had made her feel low. Even the fact that Jared had done some research on his own failed to lift her spirits.

Jared fell silent then, and Kendall turned away to gather her backpack and coat. As she moved, she missed the contemplative expression that settled on his handsome features. If she'd seen it, she may have wondered why he was watching her so closely.

Chapter Eight

Kendall had to admit that Jared was right about what she read before going to sleep affecting her dreams. The next night, when she showed up just as Jared had been about to leave to go get her, causing him to scowl at her, all she brought with her to read was a paperback novel.

It was a western saga with cowboys, Indians, saloon girls and bank robbers. That night Kendall dreamed she was in the Old West, being pursued by a masked bandit. When she woke up and related the dream, she described everything in detail except for the bandit, whom she refused to delineate. He had obviously been Jared.

Larry had called and requested a couple of extra days, which Jared had apparently given him, because he wasn't back until her Friday session. Kendall was glad to see his sun-burned face. Being able to concentrate on something other than how swiftly her feelings for Jared were growing made her relax a little.

Seeing Larry ease carefully into his chair on Friday night, Kendall couldn't resist teasing him. "Ever heard of sunscreen?"

Larry groaned. "One day. I forgot one day and I got zapped."

"So, other than that—" Kendall laughed "—how was your break?"

"It was typical. Party, party, party. Beer, beer, beer. Girls, girls, girls. Rock and roll, rock and roll, rock and roll."

"Too bad you didn't have any fun," Kendall drawled.

"Yeah, next time I'll have to try harder. How was your break? Oops, I forgot. You had to stay here with Dr. Demento."

"Sure was nice of Dr. Demento to let you have a couple of extra days for your break, wasn't it?"

Larry grinned sheepishly. "He's a prince. I thought he'd chew me out, but he actually seemed glad to give me the time. I had just gotten the burn, see, and I knew I would've been no good to him here, anyway."

Kendall wondered why Jared had been glad to give Larry extra time, since that meant he had to do extra work, but she didn't dwell on it. School was back in session on Monday, and Kendall was grateful to be busy again. Having had a week to think about Jared and her dishonest behaviour hadn't been good for her. She was having trouble sleeping even when she wasn't being watched by Jared.

Monday night she was once again engrossed in evaluating the surveys for her project. Sitting at the dining-room table, Kendall wasn't aware that someone had knocked on the door until she heard footsteps on the hardwood floor of the dining room.

Looking up, her eyes widened and she quickly looked at her watch. "It's only nine forty-five."

Jared just stood there and grinned at her. "I was just in the neighborhood and decided to drop by."

Kendall glared at him. "I told you I could take care of myself for the five minutes it takes to walk from here to the lab."

Sitting in the chair next to hers, Jared didn't look in the least repentant. "And I told you I didn't like your taking unnecessary risks. You have any coffee?"

It was futile to argue with him, Kendall concluded, and pointed over her shoulder. "It's in the kitchen, next to the coffeemaker."

Several minutes later, he was back with a mug of coffee and he settled himself next to her again. After about thirty seconds, Kendall knew there was no way she could concentrate with Jared sitting so close. So she stacked her evaluation forms and put them into their folder. Then she turned to find Jared watching her.

"Don't do that."

His eyebrows rose. "What?"

"Watch me like I'm a specimen. I don't mind it at the lab, because I *am* a specimen there, and I can't see you. But here it makes me uncomfortable."

"I'm not watching you because you're a specimen, Kendall. I'm just looking at you because you're a beautiful woman."

Kendall's lips parted to form an O and then a blush stained her cheeks deep pink. "Stop it," she ordered, although her voice lacked any conviction at all.

"Why? You *are* beautiful. Harpo's right, you know. You are a sexy number."

The mention of his sneaky bird brought a frown to Kendall's brow. "Umm, has Harpo learned to say anything else?"

Jared nodded and Kendall held her breath. "He can now say my name, as well as yours. And for some reason, he can whistle the opening themes from a couple of game shows."

Kendall feared her smile might reveal too much of her relief that the bird hadn't given her away, so she stood and gathered her work in her arms. "I'll go file these and be right out."

"Take your time," he said. "I'll just talk with Chloe in the living room for a while."

Wondering if he had something specific he was planning to discuss with Chloe, Kendall made a mental note to make sure her roommate told her everything she and Jared talked about. Then she hurried down the hall to her bedroom and collected her overnight things and crammed them into her pack, along with a science-fiction novel Chloe had given her.

Getting back as quickly as she could, Kendall slowed down at the end of the hall and sauntered into the room. Chloe and Jared were sitting on the sofa talking quietly.

Jared saw her and rose, as Chloe turned and smiled innocently. They didn't look as if they'd been discussing anything more interesting than the television listings. Which, of course, made Kendall wonder what they were up to. Then she immediately castigated herself for being paranoid.

"Ready?" he said.

Kendall nodded and went to get her coat from the closet. He took it from her and held it for her, his fingers accidentally brushing her neck several times. If she hadn't been longing for his touch, she might have moved away. It was bad enough that she'd made a resolution to stick to her rule, but now that she'd found out what being held and kissed by Jared was like, it was much more difficult to do.

"See you tomorrow, Chloe," she said, looking back at her roommate. Chloe just gave a little wave and a smile.

Out on the street they walked in silence for about a block. Then Jared spoke quietly. "Kendall, I need to ask you something."

Not feeling very confident from his tone, Kendall nevertheless said, "Ask away."

"Do your dreams vary as far as detail and strength go? Or are they all pretty much the same as to degree of vividness and similarity to reality"

Kendall felt a knot form in her stomach. Was he aware of how much she'd fudged her dreams. Had he realized that he played a starring role in so many of them? "I guess they vary some. Some are stronger than others. I can remember some even now and others I forget as soon as I wake up. Why?"

"Because you seem to be exceptionally adapted to dream research. Your recollection rates are higher than average and so is your description of detail. Added to that is the fact that you seem particularly suited to the control aspect of the project."

"I am?"

"Yes. Your dreams are affected a great deal by what you think during the day, and what you do right before sleeping. More so than other people, your mind seems to accept outside physical commands and subliminal influences. And the fact that you are precognitive is especially interesting."

Kendall didn't feel as if she was being praised. "I get the idea that there's a 'but' that hasn't been mentioned."

Even though they had reached the lab, Jared didn't unlock the door. He leaned back on his heels and gazed at her, his face blending into the shadows. "But...there's too much inconsistency. You describe some dreams in minute detail, except for one person or thing that's fuzzy. Or sometimes you start to describe something in detail, then become haphazard and the details muddy.''

Kendall felt the knot in her stomach grow bigger and tighter. "Oh. I guess that's bad, huh?''

Jared sighed in what sounded like frustration. "It's not necessarily as much bad as it is paradoxical. It's almost as if you're blocking something out. Actually that's a theory I've considered. And I have to say I was hoping you'd have a precognitive dream that manifested itself while you were on the project.''

Feeling like the lowest form of humanity for deceiving him, Kendall still couldn't bring herself to admit that she'd had so many dreams—so many *erotic* dreams—of Jared. "Am I ruining your project?''

"No,'' he said quickly. "Of course not. In fact, you're probably the most interesting subject. Because, as I said, in spite of the discrepancies in your recall, which I'm trying to figure out, you seem particularly adept at influencing your dreams. So, tonight, we're going to try something new.''

Kendall wasn't sure she was ready to try something new. But as Jared turned and unlocked the door, she shrugged and followed him down into the lab. What could happen? *A lot*—if her imagination was let loose. Too much, in fact.

Larry was talking with an older man when they came in. When he saw Jared, the man stepped forward. "Dr. Dalton, is there any reason I can't leave a light on all night? I've been coming down here and dreaming for you for over a month, and overall, it hasn't been so bad, but I hate waking up in total darkness.''

Jared considered this. "I don't see why that would be a problem, Mr. Wallace. Are you sure you can sleep with a light on?''

The man grinned. "I was just thinking about a little night-light. Nothing too bright."

"Go ahead, then," Jared said. "It may be interesting to see if it affects what you dream or how much you can recall."

Mr. Wallace and Larry then disappeared into the middle bedroom. Kendall lingered in the lab. "You know, I never even asked you before, but how many people are involved in this project?"

Jared flipped the middle monitor on and adjusted a few dials. "There are twenty-one subjects. Seven come here three times a week, seven twice, seven once a week. Each group goes through the same basic program, but I want to find out how much being in regularly controlled circumstances affects the ability to control dreams."

Kendall wondered why it was that she ended up in the three-times-a-week group. "And how much does it affect that ability?"

"So far, quite a bit. But you shouldn't be delving so deeply into my research. You're supposed to be an ignorant subject, trustingly allowing me to lead you through it all."

Kendall let her eyes go wide and vacant. "Oh, yeah. Right, Dr. Dalton. No problem—"

"Shut up." Jared laughed and pointed toward the wildflower bedroom. "And get in there."

She did, but when she got there, she realized he had followed her. Leaving the door open, he watched while she retrieved the clipboard and filled out the form on it. Taking that, he then leaned against the doorjamb and said, "All right, tonight I want you to do a little meditating before you sleep. Think about something specific—some problem you'd like to resolve, or question you'd like answered.'' Then he chuckled. "But please, no more worrying about your project."

Propping her hands on her hips, Kendall declared, "I can't help the fact that my mind has been taken over by my research. That's the way it's supposed to be. Although the research itself isn't giving me any problems."

"Then what is bothering you?"

"The thought that it won't be acceptable to the grant committee. The possibility that something else could go wrong between now and the day it's due. I could go on, but I don't want to work myself into an ulcer."

Jared shook his head. "If you didn't have any worries you'd go out and borrow some, wouldn't you."

Having no choice but to admit she was probably getting carried away, Kendall nodded. "Probably. But anticipating trouble generally helps me be prepared for it."

"Have you always been such a worrywart?"

"No. I'm normally a lot more easygoing. I'm an Aquarius, as you know. But this past year I've had too much to do that was important and that had far-reaching ramifications. Those sorts of things tend to make you consider every action as potentially helpful or damaging. Trying to make sure they come out positive instead of negative takes a lot of worrying."

"Well, tonight give it a rest and think about something else. Think of a problem—it doesn't have to be major— and tell yourself to dream a solution. Do you ever meditate?"

Kendall nodded. "I do yoga several mornings a week. Meditation is a part of it. Although I usually try not to think at all then. Just relax and try to release the tension."

"Good." Jared nodded. "Use those same techniques, only concentrate on your problem and tell yourself to dream a solution."

"What if I don't?"

He smiled. "Then we'll go on to something else."

He left the room, shutting the door behind him. Kendall wondered which of her myriad worries should be chosen for tonight's experiment. Determining to pick one that didn't involve Jared, she headed toward the bathroom.

Sitting on the bed thirty minutes later, Kendall was still trying to decide what to meditate on. The vast majority of her problems revolved around her work. Wanting to avoid anything that might bring Jared into her dreams yet again, Kendall found herself stumped.

Her family life was healthy and normal, so there was nothing there to resolve. In fact, if it weren't for her fears for her project and the fact that she was dangerously close to falling in love with a man she'd told herself was off limits, she would be remarkably content.

Her closest friend was Chloe and they had always gotten along. Kendall tried not to think about how much she was going to miss Chloe when her roommate married and moved out. Kendall knew that she'd probably have to find a new place, too, since the house was really too big for only her.

Something niggled at Kendall's brain. What was it? She and Chloe would both be moving and—Boris! Good grief, what were they going to do about Boris? Chloe had said once that they would have to toss a coin when they moved to see who would have to take Boris with them.

They'd been adopted by Boris the day he had presented himself on their doorstep and had refused to leave. The two young women had taken him in because his loud meowing was causing the neighbors to threaten to call the pound. Besides, since Kendall had dreamed him, it seemed rude not to take him in.

Now, because they'd both grown to love Boris, Kendall didn't know what they would do. He would probably be happy with either of them, although not likely as fat.

Deciding that Boris was a good enough problem to try to resolve, Kendall turned out the light and let herself relax as she sat cross-legged on the bed. Relaxing her muscles, especially the tension-filled cords of her neck, she visualized the tension leaving her body with every breath she exhaled. On every inhalation, she sent warmth to every part of her body.

She then lay down and concentrated on Boris, Chloe and herself. Telling herself to dream about who would take Boris when Chloe married and they both moved, Kendall tried to block out all other thoughts. The deep breathing she'd started became natural as she repeated her instructions to herself over and over....

Boris, his fluffy, mottled gray tail in the air, was walking confidently along the top of a narrow rail fence. Only the fence wasn't outside. It was stretched across the living room of their house.

Chloe stood on one side of the fence and Kendall stood on the other. Neither of them spoke, and they both remained still, watching the cat. Looking from side to side, Boris didn't seem to be in any great hurry to make a decision. He merely studied each of them and yawned greatly. Then his body tensed and he sank down into a crouch, his feline eyes narrowing on Kendall.

Only something was wrong. Boris looked the way he did whenever he spotted a butterfly or a bird in the backyard. He was acting like a predator. Not that he could ever catch anything, because he was too fat and slow.

Just then, though, Boris launched himself at Kendall. Fearing his sharp claws and teeth, she dodged him, only to

find out that she wasn't his target. Behind her she heard a
fluttering of wings and a startled squawk. Turning quickly,
she saw Harpo flapping his dark pink wings and looking
for a place to land. But he didn't have a tree, so he landed
on Kendall's shoulder.

Boris, in the meantime, had landed silently and was sit-
ting at Kendall's feet, looking up at Harpo and licking his
chops.

"Kendall!" Harpo squawked. He sounded desperate,
Kendall thought. And not a little indignant.

Chloe walked around the fence and picked up Boris,
who seemed disappointed. Chloe smiled at Kendall.
"Come and visit us whenever you want. Only don't bring
Harpo. Boris might get lucky next time."

Chloe returned to her side of the fence, and kept back-
ing up. The living room seemed to go on forever. Kendall
was trying to tell Chloe that Harpo wasn't hers, and that
he shouldn't be the deciding factor. But Chloe was so far
away that she couldn't hear.

Kendall turned her head to look at Harpo with con-
fused eyes. "What are you doing here?" she asked him.

Dark brown beady eyes just stared at her. Then he
squawked, "Kendall loves Jared!"

She awoke with a start and lay there blinking in the dark,
hoping against hope that she didn't talk in her sleep.

"Kendall?"

Jared's soft voice over the intercom reminded her that
she was expected to relate her dream.

"I, uh, I wanted to dream who was going to keep Boris
when Chloe gets married and moves," she began. She
closed her eyes and began relating the dream. The only
difference was that she ended it when Chloe backed away.
The rest wasn't important, anyway.

When she was finished, Jared told her that it was 1:20 a.m. and for her to relax and go back to sleep. Kendall turned onto her side and wondered if that wasn't easier said than done. The dream lingered in her mind and she wasn't at all sure of its meaning.

All of the other dreams she'd had were reasonably easy to interpret. But this one was confusing. Chloe had taken Boris because he was a cat and liked to chase birds. But since Harpo wasn't her bird, Kendall couldn't figure out why he'd even been in the dream. Jared would probably think she was being inconsistent again.

Her last conscious thought was that if Jared gave her a hard time about it, she would tell him to buzz off and get out of her dreams and take his pink bird with him.

If she had any more dreams that night—and according to experts she must have—Kendall didn't remember them. She awoke at a little after seven and stared into the utter blackness of the room, thinking that maybe Mr. Wallace was right about the night-light.

Turning over, she reached out and snapped on the lamp. The brightness of the sixty-watt bulb made her drop her face back into her pillow.

"Good morning, Kendall," Jared's voice said.

Kendall's reply was muffled.

His chuckle floated around her. "All right, I get it. You've got an hour to get up and dressed. Breakfast will be waiting for you."

More muffles were all he got in reply.

Then Kendall realized that she had a whole hour to get up and shower and dress. What a luxury. Most of the mornings she awoke here she only had half that. So she took a long leisurely shower and did her hair and makeup without having to hurry.

Emerging from the bedroom about fifteen minutes before eight, she was disappointed to find that Jared wasn't around. There was only Larry, leaning back in his chair, his feet stretched out before him, his tired eyes watching one of the monitors.

Kendall was disappointed, but scolded herself and made sure Larry didn't notice anything. "Good morning," she said cheerfully.

Larry waved and yawned. "For you maybe. You just had eight hours of sleep."

Mr. Wallace woke up and interrupted them. He began telling of the dream he'd just had in his scratchy morning voice. Apparently he'd been trying to dream up a way to persuade his brother-in-law to get out of his basement, but instead he'd had a nightmare about being chased through thigh-high weeds by a runaway lawnmower.

Larry then told Mr. Wallace what time it was and turned off the monitor. He glanced over at Kendall after he made a few notes.

"So, how's the project coming? Going to win the grant?"

"It's coming along well, and I have no idea if I'll win or not," Kendall answered.

"I'm still surprised you got Jared to agree to be a part of your work. I once heard him say that astrology was a joke and that anyone could manipulate it to suit his or her purposes."

Kendall didn't like hearing that, but plenty of people had told her the same thing. "Did he? When?"

Larry squinted as he thought. "Last year, I guess. It was during one of his classes. He was lecturing on parapsychology and someone asked about astrology. He just seemed very skeptical and said he wondered if it was a science at all. And now, just a few hours ago, he was 'evaluating' my sign traits. I couldn't believe it. He actually got into it.''

"Maybe he just needed to study some evidence," Kendall suggested, hoping she didn't sound too pleased.

"Could be." Larry nodded. "He certainly didn't give you much guff about it, even from the beginning. But then, he needed you for this project, didn't he? Seems like you both got a good deal. You convinced a skeptic that there might be something to astrology, after all, and he got a great dreamer for his experiment. He's been really pleased by you—at least most of the time."

Kendall swallowed and looked away. Even Larry thought she was doing a great job—most of the time. He thought it wasn't her fault that her dreams went haywire sometimes. Kendall rubbed her temples absently. She was getting a headache.

Mr. Wallace emerged from the middle bedroom, and after a few pleasantries, he left. Before the door could shut behind him, Jared was coming through it, carrying the food.

"Hey," Larry said, smiling and reaching for some of the bags. "What took you so long?"

"There was more of a line than usual at the restaurant," Jared explained, dropping the rest of the bags onto the desk and shrugging out of his coat.

Larry took one of the bags and snagged his coat from the rack. "Sorry I can't stay, but I have to be getting home. I'll eat on the way. See you Monday night, Jared."

Nodding, Jared didn't notice the morose expression on Kendall's face. She toyed absently with a plastic fork as she wrestled with her conscience.

No matter how much she fought with herself over it, one thing wasn't going to change. She was deceiving Jared and in the process was likely jeopardizing his research. What

Kendall had to decide was whether the preservation of her pride was worth the loss of her self-esteem. Whatever she did, she wasn't likely to come out of it happy.

She jerked back in surprise when Jared snapped his fingers in front of her eyes. "Yoo-hoo, where have you been?"

"I'm sorry." She laughed, although her apology sounded stilted even to her. "I was just thinking about something. It's not important."

Jared had set all the food out and was now pulling the plastic top off his coffee. "It had to have been at least interesting to command that kind of concentration."

He was waiting expectantly for her to say something, and Kendall was drawing a blank in the excuses department. Finally thinking of something that was safe, she said, "I was just remembering my dream about Boris. I wonder if it'll really end up that way. What happened in my dream, I mean."

Jared ate a few bites of food before answering. "I guess only time will tell for sure."

"Yes," Kendall murmured. It didn't take her mind off her troubles, but it was better than brooding in front of Jared. "I just wish I knew why Harpo was in it."

"Time will explain that, too," Jared stated patiently. "Now, eat your breakfast."

Kendall ate, but she didn't taste the food. She wanted to talk to Jared, to tell him everything, but she couldn't bring herself to do it. *I'm a coward,* she thought disgustedly. *And a selfish one at that.* Kendall decided glumly that it was just as well she had her stupid rule. Because once he found out what she'd been hiding from him, Jared wouldn't want to see her anymore, anyway.

"There you go again," Jared said.

"I'm sorry—again." Kendall sighed. "But I've been trying to figure out what the next phase in the experiment is going to be."

So it was a little white lie. She was wondering if perhaps a dream could tell her how to handle telling Jared the truth.

"More of the same, actually. I want to see if you can manage any consistency with controlling your dreams. Last night's attempt was a success, but as you know, once does not a theory prove."

Kendall nodded. "I guess that means I'll have to come up with another problem to solve."

"If your problems are all as innocuous as the one you dreamed about last night," Jared said, "then you must, indeed, be a very well-adjusted and together lady."

Torn between laughing and crying at that statement, Kendall did neither. "Well, you said I couldn't use my work, although the research itself has never given me many problems."

"Just the flak you get about its contents?"

She nodded. "If it weren't for the negativism directed at my choice of research material, I wouldn't have had a care throughout the whole process."

"Ahh, but haven't you heard that adversity builds character?"

Laughing as Jared kept a straight face, Kendall said, "I guess I have, but I hadn't thought about it recently. As far as character building goes, I preferred the Girl Scouts."

"So that's why you're so wholesome and good-natured."

Kendall managed to laugh with him, but wondered gloomily how, in only six short weeks, she'd managed to go from an easygoing professor with a project on the brink of success to an anxiety-ridden professor on the brink of disaster.

Chapter Nine

The next week was a busy one, and Jared found himself spending more and more time in his lab. With the deadline for the grant competition in just a few weeks, he was entering the final phase of his experiments.

In addition, he was performing his role in Kendall's project. She had given him a batch of surveys to evaluate, and Jared had discovered that it was interesting and challenging to test his knowledge of astrology. This was what he was currently engrossed in, and his attention kept straying as he caught himself thinking more and more about the creator of the thesis instead of the actual surveys.

Kendall had been acting very strangely lately, Jared thought as he leaned back in his office chair and stared unseeingly at the rows of books above the desk. Ever since...ever since the morning after the first night they'd tried the control experiment. She had done so well that night.

Unfortunately, subsequent attempts at the same control had failed. Kendall's dreams had been disjointed and had taken on a surreal quality that hadn't been present before. And he thought that they frightened her sometimes, although she never actually said that they did.

The sound of the door opening brought his eyes around to focus on Larry. "You're here early," he said to Jared.

It was only seven, Jared saw as he glanced at his watch. They normally didn't get to the lab until around eight. "I had work to do."

Larry's eyes scanned the desk and lit on the surveys Jared was working on for Kendall. "Are you really convinced that her theory has merit?"

Jared pushed the papers away and looked up at his assistant. "I don't know. One thing she has convinced me of, though, is that there is more to astrology than I'd thought. Some of this—" he gestured at the notes "—has some real possibilities. I'm just not sure how much of it can be used for practical purposes in clinical work."

Larry chuckled as he hung up his coat. "That's a lot more credit than you would have given the notion a few months ago."

"That's why it's always a good idea to keep an open mind."

"Right. I know that if it wasn't for you, she probably wouldn't have been able to get into the grant competition. You think the committee will take her research seriously? With the deadline only a few weeks away, I guess you're all wondering what they'll do."

Jared frowned. "Maybe that's why she's seemed so distant lately. Have you noticed?"

"I've noticed that she's been totally out of it the past few sessions. I don't have my doctorate yet, but she seems overly anxious and distracted. I think her nerves are shot, too. Are you sure her project is going well? Maybe it's fallen apart in the final stages and so has she."

Afraid much of what Larry had said was true, Jared narrowed his gaze in concentration. "But if that's true, why wouldn't she say something? She's told me more than once that her research hasn't given her any trouble. So it must be something else. If we knew what . . ."

Larry shrugged. "Maybe she has personal problems. Maybe her love life's hit the skids. Maybe you should ask her."

"I did," Jared said absently.

"Oh? What did she say?"

Jared didn't think his and Kendall's personal life was any of Larry's business, but since Larry was working on the dream project, he deserved some sort of answer. "She said she had some things she had to work out and that she would try to put them out of her mind while she was here."

Larry just shook his head and went into the lab. Jared thought about what he had offered as possible excuses for Kendall's erratic dream patterns of late. That she had personal problems was a definite probability. That she was worried about the validity of her thesis was a definite negative. That her love life was to blame . . . Jared didn't like to think that he was the cause of her problems, but he hated the idea that another man might be.

The vehemence of his thoughts took him by surprise. Having been so easygoing where women were concerned, Jared wasn't used to feeling possessive. He wasn't used to caring what women did when they weren't with him, and he wasn't used to caring about what they thought and felt. He was usually so absorbed in his work that he frequently forgot dates and apparently important things like birthdays. It wasn't that he didn't care about the women he dated; it was just that he didn't care enough for them to make a difference in his own life.

Until now. Now, Jared couldn't stop thinking about Kendall. He wondered what was worrying her and why she wouldn't talk to him about it. He wondered where she was right now. He wondered when he'd ever get the chance to be with her without so many outside forces tugging at them. He wondered who would believe him when he said that he really hadn't had any intention of falling in love with her.

"The way things have been going the past several days," he muttered to himself, "it doesn't look like it will matter."

He understood Kendall's reasons for not wanting to get romantically involved with a man she worked with. Especially after what she'd been through last year. *But this is different,* he thought stubbornly. *This is me.*

"You were right, Cynthia," he said quietly to himself. "It took someone very special for me to fall in love. Unfortunately, I don't know if she's willing to give us a chance."

"I say tell him," Chloe stated firmly. "And the sooner the better. Tonight."

Kendall stuffed her completed evaluations into her backpack with her overnight things and zipped it shut. "If I thought he wouldn't get angry and yell and hate me for it, I might."

"Think about what you just said, Kendall. Jared Dalton is a scientist who researches the workings of the human mind. Don't you think it might be a little out of character for him to go off the deep end and start yelling at you in his lab?"

Kendall hadn't thought of it exactly like that. "Maybe he wouldn't yell—but he'd still probably hate me."

Chloe was not swayed. "I believe that, if you explain everything that's happened and tell him how you feel, he will look before he leaps down your throat. Besides, if you don't get this resolved you'll wear your nerves to a frazzle."

"I know." Kendall sighed and sank onto the sofa. "For the past week I've been a total flop in the dream department. When I can remember the dreams I have, they're totally weird. Like Salvatore Dali painted them."

"Just tell Jared all about it, and I'll bet you'll be able to exert control over the dreams again."

"I don't know, Chloe. Maybe after we all finish the evaluations and—"

"Don't let this opportunity pass you by, Kendall. Get all of this off your chest. And while you're at it, tell Jared you're in love with him."

Kendall's laugh sounded disbelieving. "Right. You'd have me stripped down to my emotional bones, wouldn't you?"

"Better than letting doubt gnaw away at you. And I hate to leave, but Brice should be here any minute. The showing at the gallery starts in fifteen minutes, and if we get there late all the wine and cheese will be gone."

A few minutes later Brice had knocked on the door, and he and Chloe went out, leaving Kendall alone to ruminate. Maybe what Chloe said made sense. After all, Jared had the right to know she was possibly ruining his experiment.

Kendall could no longer deny that she was in love with Jared. Chloe knew it. And if she was honest with herself, Kendall had known it for longer than she wanted to think about. Even Harpo, the loud cockatoo, knew it. But he'd better not have said anything to Jared, Kendall threatened mentally. She was in love with Jared and she would find a way to let him know everything herself! She didn't need a pink bird to tell him for her.

By the time Jared knocked on the door an hour later, Kendall had rehearsed a dozen different approaches to telling him, but none seemed right. Hoping that something would come to her before her determination wavered, she pulled open the door and smiled up at him.

"Come on in. I'm ready. I just have to get my coat."

Jared was watching her with wary eyes when she turned back to face him. "Are you all right?"

Trying not to grimace, Kendall nodded. "I'm fine, I guess. I've been trying to deal with a problem, and it's just gone from bad to worse."

Swiftly zipping up her coat and slinging her pack over one shoulder, Kendall waited for Jared to open the door, but for a moment he just looked at her. "I'm a good listener," he said quietly.

She knew he was serious, and she merely nodded. "I hope you still think so later."

Jared's eyes bored into hers for another moment before he nodded and opened the door. The weather had turned balmy and Kendall was glad winter was over. Spring was her favorite time of year and she wasn't enjoying this one nearly as much as she would have liked to.

They were almost to the entrance to the lab before Jared spoke. "Does this problem you mentioned have anything to do with why your sessions here have gone awry?"

Kendall nodded hesitantly. Her biggest disappointment in this whole mess had been her failure to do well in Jared's project. She might actually have been able to help him prove his theories valid if her dreams hadn't so often been of him. And then she had to fall in love with him, making her fear of his rejection overwhelm and short-circuit her emotion. It had gotten to the point where she could hardly meditate into relaxation to get to sleep, much less perform well in his experiment.

"Yes, I guess it does," she said. "It's all very complicated and I should have told you about it before, but I was afraid to."

Jared paused as he pulled open the door. "Afraid of me?"

Kendall smiled sadly in the darkness. "In a way."

Without giving him time to start asking the inevitable questions, she slipped inside and started down the stone stairway. She knew when Jared followed by listening for his footsteps. He'd only paused a moment, she thought as she entered the lab and let her pack slide down her arm.

Tossing it onto the floor next to the door to the wildflower bedroom, she shrugged out of her coat and hung it up as Jared entered the lab. He placed his coat alongside hers and then gestured for her to sit.

He pulled his chair to the corner of the desk, so that their knees were practically touching. Holding her barely steady gaze for a moment, he said, "So, why are you afraid of me?"

Kendall winced, then asked, "Larry isn't coming in tonight, is he?"

Jared shook his head slowly. "No, he's off tonight."

One thing she didn't need was an audience. "Oh. Good."

"Kendall, what is it? It's disconcerting, to say the least, to think that after all these weeks you say you're afraid of me. Did I do something?"

"No," she told him hastily. "It's me. Jared, I'm sorry. I didn't mean for any of this to turn out this way. It just isn't fair to you and I don't blame you if you get mad."

Jared smiled in confusion. "Why would I be mad at you? What isn't fair?"

"It isn't fair that you've done so well in my project and I've messed yours up."

Now he looked surprised. "No, you haven't."

Kendall jumped to her feet. "Yes, I have. And even though I really didn't mean your project any harm, the end result is the same."

Jared rose slowly and reached out to grasp her upper arms and pull her toward him. "Kendall, if this is what you've been so upset about, I wish you would just forget it. You've really done quite well in the tests—for the most part. If you've worked yourself into this anxiety over the fact that you think you haven't done well enough, then it's no wonder your dreams have reflected that feeling. I'll put that in my report findings, too."

This was not going the way she had planned it, Kendall thought. Jared had now pulled her into his arms and was rubbing her back soothingly. Tilting her head to look at him, she was about to give it another try, but forgot what she was going to say when she looked into his eyes.

He leaned down and kissed her, and she didn't even think of pushing him away. This might very well be the last kiss they ever shared, and Kendall wasn't about to deny herself the pleasure she found in his arms. When the kiss finally ended, she leaned against Jared, not wanting to think of anything but how she felt at that moment. She loved Jared and it was almost as if he loved her, she thought as she rested her cheek against his chest, listening to his heartbeat.

"Kendall," he said, his voice low and rumbling through his chest, "I hope this doesn't make you angry, but I think that your rule is stupid. Isn't this more important?"

She nodded against his chest. "Yes, it is. I should have known that rule would never be able to stand up to you."

Besides that, she thought, her rule was now a moot point. Since she'd fallen in love with Jared, it was too late for her.

Leaning back, she looked up at him. "Jared, I—"

"No more placing blame, Kendall. Especially on yourself. Now, why don't you get in there and go to sleep? Now that you know I don't blame you for anything, maybe we can get something accomplished again."

"But, Jared—" she began.

"But nothing. It wasn't your fault. It wasn't as if you did it on purpose."

Kendall suddenly shivered, feeling an icy chill that began inside her radiating outward. "I, uh, guess you'd be really mad if I had done it on purpose?"

"Yes, I would be. Now, here," he picked up her backpack and handed it to her. As she started to turn toward the room, she felt his hand on her arm. She raised her eyes slowly to look at him. "Don't forget to try to dream a solution to a problem," he said softly.

Kendall wondered how she would be able to pick just one.

"I'll try," she managed.

"Don't make it too complicated," he suggested. "Something like what to get your dad for his birthday or what kind of car you should buy. You really should get one, you know."

"I know, but since I only live a few blocks from campus, I thought I'd just save my money."

There were flickers of desire in his dark eyes as she looked at him, but there was also challenge.

"Why don't you stop worrying so much and let whatever is going to happen just happen?"

Kendall's smile was slightly sardonic. "Maybe I'm afraid that I won't like what's going to happen."

"Maybe you will," he returned, and kissed her swiftly.

Kendall went into the bedroom and closed the door behind her. What on earth was she going to do now?

After an hour of indecision, Kendall decided to try to dream where she would spend her vacation this summer. She didn't feel like vacationing in the least, but it was the tamest thing she could think of at the moment.

Settling onto the bed in a cross-legged position, Kendall wondered if tonight would be another disaster or if she would manage to get a grip on her dreams. Her whole confession attempt had been a flop and she had chickened out at the end. Especially after Jared had said that he really would be angry if she had messed up on purpose.

But she hadn't done it on purpose, she told herself. Even if the end result was the same. Sighing in defeat, Kendall reasserted her resolve to tell Jared before she left in the morning. Then, putting forth her most determined effort to relax and concentrate, Kendall drifted to sleep asking herself where she should vacation this summer.

She was warm—deliciously warm. A slight breeze just barely tickled the bare skin of her arms. The sun was setting over the water and Kendall was watching it disappear in a brilliant display of color.

Looking up, she saw palm leaves swaying gently above her. She was walking along a beach and she could feel the white sand under her bare feet. She was wearing some sort of short red-and-purple skirt that tied around her hips and a matching halter top. When she reached up to push her hair out of her eyes, she realized that she had a flower in her hair. Looking over her shoulder for a moment, she saw

*some sort of house hidden in the foliage. With a sudden
surge of energy, she ran down the beach, stopping every
once in a while to pick up a shell and examine it.*

*She was happy. She had no worries and nothing weighed
on her conscience. It was a wonderful feeling. She started
to sing. The tune was familiar, but the words weren't clear,
so she couldn't place the song.*

*Another shell, this one large and pink, lay just ahead.
She reached out and touched it. Seeing her hand stretched
out, she suddenly realized that she was wearing a wedding
ring.*

*She was married? But this was supposed to be her va-
cation. The images became confusing and hazy. Where
was she? Was she dreaming about herself? If she was married, where was her husband?*

The dream faded gently and Kendall realized that she
was awake. Grateful that she hadn't dreamed another
study in surrealism, but disappointed that she hadn't accomplished what she'd intended, Kendall cleared her
throat.

"Uh . . . I had intended to dream where I would be going on my vacation this summer, but I don't think I did."

She then described the setting—the palm trees, the
ocean, the sand and the shells. After describing her clothes
and the flower in her hair, she hesitated.

"Kendall? Is that all?"

"No, but this is where it got weird. I was singing something, but I can't remember the song. And I was wearing
a wedding ring."

A silence filled the room. "You were? Was there a man
in the dream?"

"No. I didn't see him. But I got the feeling he was in the
house behind me. It was then that things faded on me."

"Okay. Listen, can you remember the song? Think about it."

Kendall closed her eyes and tried to put herself back on that tropical beach. The song—it was so familiar. She could hear the melody. She hummed, hoping the words would come to her.

Jared was laughing.

"What's so funny?" Kendall asked.

"You. That song. It sounds like 'Tiny Bubbles' to me."

Kendall blinked in the darkness. It was "Tiny Bubbles." She giggled softly. "I guess I was in Hawaii."

"I guess so. That was actually very good. It's only two-thirty, so try to get some more sleep."

Kendall murmured good-night to him and turned over. She didn't know why he thought she'd done a good job when she hadn't dreamed what she'd intended to. And who had she married? She didn't want to marry anybody but Jared, and the likelihood of that happening after she told him the truth was nonexistent.

Punching her pillow at the unfairness of life, Kendall wondered what it might have been like if she and Jared didn't have all these obstacles in their way.

The second time she awoke was after another erotic dream of her and Jared frolicking in the nude. Only this time it wasn't a pond. It was in a bedroom on a bed.

Her cheeks flushing as the images flashed through her mind like a television rerun, Kendall refused to describe the dream, claiming she could only remember being in a room she didn't recognize.

Hurrying to the bathroom, she emerged thirty minutes later to find Jared sitting in his office writing on something. Hearing her behind him, he turned in his swivel chair and smiled at her. Kendall smiled in return, but was afraid that she didn't look very confident.

"I just finished," he said.

"What?"

"Your evaluations. I did most of them last night while you were sleeping. It was more interesting than I thought it would be."

He held out the sheaf of papers and Kendall took them, trying not to clench her fingers around them too tightly.

She should be feeling on top of the world right now, she thought. Instead she felt awful. She loved this man and she'd lied to him. Not just once, but over and over. Kendall knew she couldn't live with herself one more minute without telling him.

"Jared, I need to tell you something. I tried to last night, but I never did."

He rose and they went back into the larger room of the lab. Jared sat on the arm of the sofa, but Kendall was too nervous to sit. So she paced.

"Kendall, I hope this isn't about how you feel you've done in this experiment. I thought we'd—"

"You think we talked about it, Jared, but we didn't. I never did tell you what I meant to. But I have to now, because you deserve to know."

Jared must have sensed she was serious, because he just nodded and waited. Kendall, with the moment she had dreaded finally upon her, found that she was calmer than she had thought possible. "I think you realize that I really didn't want to become a part of this project, Jared, but when Chloe suggested we help each other out, I guess I thought I could overcome my . . . reservations."

"And they were?"

She looked at him and waved her free hand at him helplessly. "I didn't...that is, I...well, one thing was my precogs. I didn't want anyone to know about that."

"Why not?"

"Because when I was a little girl, my parents had me tested at the urging of a family doctor and it wasn't a pleasant experience. In the end, the psychiatrist I was taken to decided that I was lying and that I had some kind of deep emotional problem. My parents told him he was full of it and took me home. After that, I mostly just kept my dreams to myself."

"But that hasn't been a problem, has it? I mean here?"

She shook her head. "Not really. Except for the fact that I know you were hoping something I dreamed would come true."

"Yes. It's too bad that nothing has."

Kendall ran her tongue over her lips. "Actually, one did. But it wasn't a dream I dreamed here. Luck of the Irish, huh?"

Jared's eyes widened. "What did you dream?"

"I dreamed I was in your car. Then later, I was. Not very spectacular."

"Kendall, why didn't you tell me?"

Here goes, she thought ruefully. "Because of all the other dreams I'd had here that I sometimes...uh...left some details out of."

The rustling of the papers in Kendall's hands as she rolled them into a tube was the only sound in the room. Until Jared finally rose slowly and looked directly into her guilty eyes.

"You what?"

"I didn't always tell you everything that I dreamed. Mostly, I did, but sometimes I left out a person or...things that happened."

Jared was clearly confused. "But why? You know how important those descriptions are to my experiments."

"Because I was too embarrassed," she blurted, suddenly looking away.

"Embarrassed?"

Why did he have to sound so incredulous? Her eyes met his again and she nodded. "Yes, embarrassed. The thought of you, not to mention Larry, knowing what I had dreamed was enough to keep me from telling you certain details."

"But we wouldn't have made fun of you or—" Suddenly he stopped, and Kendall saw him fighting a small smile. "Oh, I think I get it. Were they, shall we say, explicit dreams?"

Kendall rolled her eyes. "They were erotic, Jared. And the thought of having to see you and Larry every day after telling you things like...well, like what I did in those dreams...was too much to ask. Even though I knew I was wrong to do it, I couldn't help it."

The smile wasn't on his lips anymore as he sighed and walked over to where she was still rolling up her surveys. "I understand your uneasiness, Kendall, but you knew how important it was that you be as accurate as possible. Why didn't you tell me later, when we were alone? Maybe we could have worked something out. Larry isn't privy to all the information I gather."

Kendall sighed. "Because I couldn't bring myself to describe those dreams to you. They were just so personal..."

"I realize that, Kendall. But I thought you trusted me enough to know that I'd never behave unprofessionally about something like that."

His voice had cooled considerably in the last few seconds, Kendall realized miserably. "It had nothing to do with that, Jared," she said.

"Then what was it? For that matter, why did you decide to tell me at all? I would never have known you'd been holding back anything consciously. Why now?"

"Because I couldn't stand it anymore," Kendall admitted. "I knew it was wrong and that it wasn't fair to you. Especially after you were so fair with me," she added, waving her rolled-up surveys at him.

"Oh, right. So your conscience finally got to you, huh?"

Kendall nodded. "Yes, I guess so. I'm sorry, and if I could make it up to you, I would." Remembering that she'd written down all of her dreams, she said, "If it would help, I—"

"Never mind. I don't really think that this is something that can be fixed."

Kendall swallowed the lump in her throat and nodded. "I'm sorry, Jared. I hope I didn't ruin the whole project."

His eyes looked bleak for a moment before he turned away. Then he looked back at her and his expression was neutral. "Right now, Kendall, my project doesn't seem to matter."

That was about the last thing Kendall had expected him to say. "But Jared, what if I—"

He held up one hand and her words stopped abruptly. "Can we not talk right now? I have a lot to think about and I'd like to go home."

Tears stung her eyes at his dismissal, but Kendall could hardly blame him. She silently collected her things and slipped through his office and up the stairs to the first floor.

Refusing to resort to sobbing in the lobby, she pushed her unhappy thoughts away and left the building. She had only an hour or so before she had to be back for her first class of the day. She would have to wait until later to fall apart.

Getting through the day was more difficult than she had anticipated. Barely able to keep her concentration on what she was teaching, Kendall was intensely grateful when her last class ended at three that afternoon.

Gathering her book bag and her coat, she practically ran the few blocks to her house and sighed with relief when the door closed behind her. Collapsing on the sofa, she expected to cry her heart out, but when no tears appeared, Kendall decided she must be in shock.

Unable to simply sit there waiting to cry, she rose and found the evaluations she and Chloe had completed. Then she pulled the sorry-looking rolled-up tube of papers Jared had finished from her backpack, along with her spiral notebook, and began to open the small, individually sealed envelopes that contained the test group's astrological signs.

She'd just opened the first envelope when Chloe walked in. "Oh, hi, Kendall. You're back early today, aren't you?"

Shaking her head, Kendall said, "Not really. I just didn't hang around the office like I usually do."

"Oh. What are you doing?"

Holding up the card, Kendall explained that she was finishing up the statistical part of her project. Chloe, anxious to see how she did, sat down on the floor next to the coffee table where Kendall had spread out her work.

"By matching the number on the top of the card in the envelope with the number at the top of each form, I'll be able to record our rate of success."

Chloe nodded. "Right." Then she looked at Kendall more closely. "Say, what's wrong? You look awful. Oh, my gosh, you told him, didn't you?"

Kendall nodded. "Well, I told him that I hadn't told him all of my dreams and that it was because I was embarrassed because they were erotic."

"What did he say?"

"Oh, he wanted to know why I hadn't trusted him to be the professional he is, and then he basically told me to get out."

Chloe was indignant. "He didn't! After you told him those dreams were about him and that you loved him on top of it? That creep. I have half a mind—"

"No, Chloe. Actually, I never got around to telling him those things."

Her roommate stared at her. "Then *you* are the one with half a mind. Why didn't you tell him?"

"Because he never gave me the chance. I told you he practically kicked me out of the lab as it was."

"Well, did you at least tell him that you'd recorded all the dreams in your journal?"

Kendall shook her head. "I started to, but . . ."

"But what?"

"But I didn't tell him. Chloe, I don't really want to discuss this now. I feel awful as it is. Maybe later I can think about it, but right now I just want to look at all of these evaluations and see how well my theory has stood up to practical application."

Chloe started to say something, then apparently changed her mind. "All right. I'll help and we'll get it done in no time."

"No time" turned out to be about two hours. The evaluations were all in neat piles and the results had been tabulated.

"Well," Chloe sighed. "There you have it. I'm still ticked off that you and Jared did better than I did."

Kendall's smile was wan. "You were only three percent behind him. You did very well."

Chloe paused and squeezed Kendall's hand. "Kendall, why aren't you happy? Why aren't you jumping for joy? You did it. You proved your thesis, and by a good margin. All of us were more than seventy-five percent accurate, for a total percentage of eighty-four percent. That's fantastic. Even if you don't win the grant, your project is a success. You're sure to get your paper on it published."

Kendall nodded and looked at the stacks of forms. "I know. I should be happy. But you know what, Chloe? It just doesn't seem to matter anymore."

Chapter Ten

Kendall stayed home alone that night, restless and unable to concentrate on anything. Her project sat finished on the dining-room table. She'd worked on it all afternoon and into the evening, but it was mostly by rote.

Why wasn't she happy, or at least relieved, that it was finished? She was sure to get a trade journal to publish it, which would mean a great deal to her career. But her victory wasn't what she'd expected it to be. In fact, she didn't even care if she won the grant competition or not.

The only thing that really mattered was Jared, she told herself. She loved him, and her happiness was hollow without him there to share it.

She went to bed early and for once didn't remember a single dream. In a way, it was a blessing not to have to remember and describe something when she woke up. But without hearing Jared's voice, her morning could hardly be called good.

At breakfast, Chloe glared at her disgustedly. "You look awful. I don't see why you don't just go and tell him how you feel. What in the world do you have to lose? Could you feel worse than you do now?"

Kendall had to admit that she probably couldn't. Later, once she got to class, even her students noticed her less than energetic performance. After turning her project into the office that afternoon, Kendall went home, uncertain about whether Jared would want her to show up that night or not.

Seeing herself as she passed by a mirror in the dining room, Kendall stared at herself. This wasn't her. This pale frightened woman wasn't Kendall Arden. Kendall Arden took responsibility for her own destiny, right or wrong. She didn't just slouch around feeling sorry for herself and hoping that her fairy godmother would touch down and fix everything the way she wanted it. Kendall Arden was no quitter and no wimp. If things didn't work out the way she hoped, at least she wouldn't be able to say she hadn't tried.

Looking at her watch, Kendall saw that it was five forty-five. Feeling determination sweep through her, she stood and reached for her coat. "Chloe, can I borrow your car?"

Hesitating for only a moment out of surprise, Chloe smiled encouragingly and nodded. "Sure. The keys are on the hook."

Digging into her backpack, Kendall retrieved her driver's license and the notebook she'd been using as her dream journal and headed for the door.

"Good luck," Chloe called.

"Thanks," Kendall said as she left. She was going to need it.

Stopping first at the university, just in case Jared had decided to come in early, Kendall went down to his office and found the door ajar. Tapping lightly on it and pushing it all the way open, she stopped and let the breath she'd been holding escape.

"Larry, what are you doing here?"

Startled, Larry was standing at the copier, placing a sheet of paper on it. "Don't do that, Kendall. You scared me. And what do you mean, what am I doing here? I work here. I got up early to come in and make a copy of a paper that's due today. I have until six o'clock to get it into Dr. Willmott's box. What are you doing here?"

"I just needed to speak to Jared about something. What time does he usually get in?"

"Usually we get in around eight. Unless there's something special we have to do. You want to leave a note?"

He gestured toward the desk and Kendall automatically went over to it. Knowing she had no intention of writing a note, she started to turn away. But just as she did, her eye caught two words printed on the front of a medium-sized composition book.

Dream journal.

Her hands were drawn to it even as her mind raced. Jared's dream journal? He'd told her once that he kept one, but she hadn't given it much thought. Knowing she was invading his privacy, but too curious to stop herself, she opened the book in the middle and let her eyes fall on the passage.

March 5—Kendall again. We were on my sailboat on the bay. Only there weren't any other boats. Just us out on the water. She went down into the galley and then returned with two drinks and no clothes on. She came toward me the way she did before with that smile that was only for me. Then we were making love, right there on the deck in the sunlight. And it was the most incredible experience I've ever had. I wonder if it would really be like that with her. I have the feeling that it would be. . . .

Kendall shut the book abruptly, her face flaming, but her heart beating faster and a curl of desire causing an ache deep inside her.

Glancing over her shoulder to where Larry still stood at the copier, Kendall surreptitiously gathered the book in her arms and hid it under her coat.

"I think I'll just call him, Larry. See you later."

"Sure," he answered.

Then she was gone, racing up the stairs and outside. When she got into Chloe's car, she paused, staring at the journal. She wanted to open and read more and see how many times Jared had dreamed of her.

But she didn't. She just started the car and determinedly steered it in the direction of Jared's house. She didn't even remember the ride out to his place, and she hoped she hadn't broken any traffic laws on the trip.

Once she'd pulled into the driveway, though, she felt her determination falter. What if he refused to listen to her? What if he threw her out?

Lifting her chin, she opened the car door. He wouldn't dare. Besides, he was a Libra and Libra's sense of justice wouldn't let her down. He would at least hear her out. After that she had no guarantees. But that was a chance she had to take—Jared was worth the risk to her pride.

Marching up to the front door, she jabbed a finger at the doorbell and waited impatiently, tapping her toe on the porch. Looking down, she realized she was still wearing the clothes she'd put on that morning. Her jeans would have been more comfortable, but her gray cashmere sweater and straight skirt would have to do. One of her gray pumps was still tapping on the porch when the door opened less than a minute later.

Her eyes swung up to meet his surprised expression. "Kendall."

"Yes, it's me. Can I come in? I wanted to tell you something. And give you something."

His surprise gave way to puzzlement, but he stepped aside and let Kendall enter. Harpo's screeching didn't catch her off guard this time.

"Go on into the living room. I have to turn off the oven, but I'll be right there."

When he left, Kendall walked right over to confront the rose-breasted cockatoo. The bird was dancing on a leaf-enshrouded branch and bobbing his head.

"Harpo, have you been blabbing? I trusted you not to, you know. I fed you nuts and kept you company that weekend. Have you now stabbed me in the back?"

"Oh, there you are," Jared said from the entrance to the living area. "If you're trying to teach him new words, you'll need a lot of luck."

Kendall turned and tried not to look hopeful. "Hasn't he learned anything else yet?"

"No. All I can get out of him is our names, the game show themes and the fact that you're a sexy number."

Looking up at his enigmatic eyes, Kendall wasn't sure how he meant that last remark. She glanced back at Harpo and smiled. She was about to pat him on his head, but he ruffled his crest at her and she decided that he wouldn't like it.

"Would you care for something to drink?"

Now he was just being polite, Kendall thought. She shook her head. "No, thanks. Actually, I came by to give you this."

She held out her dream journal, but Jared was slow in taking it.

"What is it?"

"It's a journal I kept of all those dreams I was too embarrassed to tell you about."

He took the notebook and let it rest in his hand, as if weighing it. "You didn't have to do this. I understood how you felt when you said you couldn't describe your erotic dreams. Lots of people are like that. I just thought that since we were both psychologists that you wouldn't have had the same inhibitions as most people."

Kendall nodded. "I know. And maybe I wouldn't have—if the dreams hadn't all been about you."

"You dreamed about me?"

He sounds so incredulous, she thought wryly. "Yes, I did. And I'm still embarrassed about it, but I guess I'll get over it."

Pulling out his journal, she held it up. "I went by your office a few minutes ago, in case you'd come in early. Larry was there. I was about to leave when I saw this."

He frowned and seemed a bit uncomfortable. Maybe he understood how she felt more than she'd thought. "I don't suppose you read any of it?" he said.

Kendall remembered the entry she'd seen and wondered if her cheeks would ever stop burning. "As a matter of fact, I did. But just one entry. I didn't think it was fair of me to be reading yours unless you could read mine."

Jared just stared at her. "Why did you decide to give this to me?"

"I'd always intended to give it to you," she explained. "That's why I kept it. There was simply no way I could just lie there in your lab and say aloud that I'd dreamed about . . . us. It was just too intimate, I guess. So I wrote everything down with the intention of giving it to you after I was finished with my part of your project. Then I wouldn't have to listen if you laughed at me, or see your eyes later and know that you felt sorry for me or something."

She was still wearing her jacket, and her fingers were worrying the zipper furiously. Jared dropped the two journals onto the coffee table and walked over to her, capturing her hands.

"Feel sorry for you? For having the same kinds of dreams about me that I was having about you?"

"But I didn't know that then," Kendall wailed.

Jared helped her out of her coat and nudged her toward the sofa. He hung her jacket on the brass coat tree and sighed. "Well, you should have."

Whirling to face him, Kendall gaped. "What do you mean, I should have?"

He grinned at her. "Really, Kendall, the way I took advantage of every opportunity to touch you, to kiss you, to feel your body next to mine? I thought that my desire for you was fairly obvious."

"Oh," she said and sank into the cushions of the sofa.

Jared sank down next to her, and for the first time Kendall noticed that he was wearing a CSU sweatshirt and a pair of jeans. He looked even more...masculine than usual. And Kendall was always aware of Jared as a man.

"Are you sure you wouldn't like something to drink now?"

Kendall nodded, then shook her head. "No, I'm driving. Besides, I came here to talk to you, and I'm not finished."

He quirked one eyebrow at her. "You mean there's more?"

"Yes, there's more. But if you're going to make fun of me..."

Jared's hand touched her knee. "I would never make fun of you, Kendall," he said quietly. "I think you know me better than that by now."

Kendall, her whole body aware of the spot on her knee where his hand rested, managed to keep her voice from shaking as she spoke. "Sometimes I think I've gotten to know you well, and other times I think I don't know anything."

He gazed at her for another moment, then removed his hand and leaned back. "So, what else did you want to tell me?"

"What? Oh, yeah, uh, it was about what I told you yesterday morning. I really did dream that I was riding in your car, but there was more than that. I also dreamed that we were...uh..."

"Making out?"

"Yes. But in my dream, the car was zipping along. I didn't think it would come true until...well...until we almost hit that tree."

He nodded. "Is that why you freaked out and jumped out of the car?"

"Yes. I always become a little disoriented after a dream is realized, but that was even more intense than usual."

Jared smiled slowly. "We are pretty intense together, aren't we?"

Kendall laughed nervously. "Yes, we are."

"And we're not going to pretend to ignore it anymore, are we?"

She paused, thinking about how she'd tried to deny her feelings for Jared. And how totally unsuccessful she'd been. "I don't think it would do any good, would it?"

Now Jared laughed. "No, it wouldn't. I'm relieved that you now think so, too."

There was something about the expression in his eyes that made Kendall's breath catch and her heart hope. Maybe now was the right time for her to take a real risk and tell him why she'd done all of this.

"Jared, you know there was a good reason I had that rule about not getting involved with people I worked with."

"Sure, but some rules just beg to be broken, don't they?"

"This one was doomed from the minute I met you," she whispered.

Leaning forward, Jared kissed her lightly, once. "Was it?"

"Yes, it was," Kendall managed, although her concentration was definitely slipping. "But you never even noticed me, so..."

"That's because you were always hiding from me."

"I wasn't exactly hiding." She sniffed.

He laughed. "Yes, you were. But since you were forced out by the grant competition and Chloe, it's all right. And anyway, I think I would have gotten around to finding you eventually, even if you were hiding."

"You think so?"

"Sure. What we have is so special that we would have found it no matter what."

Kendall couldn't stop herself from leaning toward him. "You really think so?"

"I'm positive. Kendall—"

A squawk from behind her startled her and she jerked away. Rising, she turned to look at Harpo, who was dancing on his perch.

"Kendall!" he shrieked at her.

"Oh, no, you don't, you ungrateful fowl. You keep your beak shut and let me do the talking."

"Kendall's a sexy number!"

She gave him a dirty look and turned back to look at Jared, who seemed amused, but bewildered.

"Why do I get the impression that you and Harpo have been holding out on me?"

Kendall laughed and gave him an exaggerated shrug. "I'm sure I have no idea what you mean. You said yourself he can't say anything else."

Jared rose and looked over her shoulder at Harpo. "Right, I did. Kendall, I—"

"Kendall!" Harpo screeched. "Kendall loves Jared!"

"Hey, he...what?"

Kendall's eyes closed. It just wasn't fair. A beautiful moment shouldn't be interrupted by a bird. Unless, she suddenly thought...unless her love for Jared was one-sided. But it couldn't be, she prayed. It wouldn't be fair. And one thing Libras were supposed to be was fair.

"Where did he pick that up? Open your eyes, Kendall. Kendall—"

"Kendall! Kendall loves Jared!"

Opening her eyes, she did an about-face to glare at Harpo. "He heard you, already, you stupid pink bird!"

Harpo whistled and danced some more. Kendall let Jared move to stand just behind her. She saw his hand reach out to gently touch Harpo's deep-pink breast.

"You wouldn't lie, would you, Harpo? Would he, Kendall?"

Kendall couldn't speak, but Harpo was in fine voice.

"Kendall loves Jared!"

"Does she?" Jared whispered into her ear.

She couldn't stop herself from answering in a whisper, "Yes, I'm afraid she does. She tried not to, but—"

"Jared loves Kendall, too."

His softly spoken words shook her to her heart. "He does?"

"Yes, he does. Very much."

"He wouldn't just say that because she did?"

Jared chuckled softly. "No, he really means it."

Relief and joy streaked through Kendall's body as she turned into his arms. "Harpo's got a big beak." She smiled. "I was going to tell you without any help from him, but I got a case of the last-second panics."

"You don't ever have to worry about that, Kendall," he assured her. "I do love you. I thought I'd never be able to love a woman more than my work. However, when I realized that I really didn't care what happened to my project but I did care whether or not you loved me, I knew I'd found the only woman who meant the entire world to me."

Kendall's eyes filled with tears as she gazed up at him. How could she have thought that she could keep herself from falling in love with this man? "I realized the same thing about my project. I finished it, by the way, and it was a success. But it didn't seem to matter, since I thought I'd screwed up any chance I might have had with you."

He shook his head. "I admit I was disappointed with you when you told me how you'd kept parts of your dreams from me, but I was more concerned that you would slip out of my life. If you hadn't shown up tonight, I would have come to your house and gotten you."

She smiled. "I was a mess for a while. But then I told myself that I had to see you and tell you everything. Then it was up to you."

"I guess I did okay, huh?"

"I'm glad you were patient with me, Jared. And I'm glad you don't hate me for ruining your experiment."

"Ruin? No way. Now that I have full disclosure from your journal, and the fact that three of your precogs have actualized, I think I'll be sitting in the catbird seat with that committee."

Frowning, Kendall corrected him. "Three? But only one has happened. And that one I didn't dream while at the lab."

"So what? You recorded it in your journal, didn't you?"

She nodded. "Yes, but that's still only one. What about the others?"

Jared's dark eyes twinkled as he rested his hands on the small of her back and kept her body resting against his. "The others will soon happen. Chloe's going to get Boris, since you'll be living here with me, and he and Harpo wouldn't get along."

"Oh." Kendall nodded, her smile widening. "I see. And what's the last one?"

"Why, the honeymoon in Hawaii, of course. We'll go there as soon as we get married, which should be just after the semester is over this summer."

"So, that was you in the house on the beach?"

"It had better not be anybody else," he growled at her. "I'm the only man you're going on a honeymoon with. Oh, uh, will you marry me?"

Kendall laughed as the happiness in her heart bubbled over. "Yes, I will. Because I wouldn't want to go on my honeymoon with anybody but you."

Desire flared in his eyes to mingle with the love Kendall had seen for herself. She knew that Jared could see the same emotions mirrored in her own eyes.

The kiss they shared then was unlike any other. His lips teased hers even as hers made promises to him.

Kendall felt his arms holding her against his hard body, and she felt safer and more loved and desired than she had ever thought was possible.

She sighed when his lips left hers to move across her cheek. "If this is a dream, Jared, please don't ever wake me up."

"Never," he breathed into her ear. "This is one dream we'll share forever."

Epilogue

The Chesapeake State University Eagle
July 1

Dr. Chloe Munson, Professor of Psychology at CSU, was pleased to announce last week that she has been given the go ahead to open a clinic for disadvantaged children in Baltimore this fall. Dr. Munson, who won the Gundersson Award for Psychological Research last month, said that the award money would be used in conjunction with other donations for the clinic, where she will use art therapy as a tool to help children who have been victims of trauma and crime.

Dr. Munson, who plans to wed Baltimore art gallery owner Brice Wilkins next month, said that she was especially grateful for the support of her fiancé and of her dear friends, fellow psychology professors Jared and Kendall Dalton, who were recently married and are honeymooning in Hawaii. Dr. Munson also said that the newlyweds were planning to donate their time to her new clinic upon their return to the university.

"Psychologists like the Daltons are very special," she said. "They study not only the mind, but the heart as well."

MORE ABOUT
THE LIBRAN MAN

by Lydia Lee

Without a doubt, Libras are the most charming men of the Zodiac. They're also renowned for being the most handsome, the most fair and alas, probably the most maddening, as those of you who've been ensnared by their legendary smiles know. This man's occasional inability to make a decision, however, isn't really the end of the world, it's just that, sometimes, it feels that way. As flaws go, it's in the minor leagues, but, still, at times it can get downright annoying. The solution? Gently take the reins and make the decision yourself. So, what's with this indecisive charmer, anyway? Simply put, he has this uncanny ability to see both sides of any issue and having the scales of justice for his symbol, he balances one side against the other, ever striving for the Right Answer. He abhors anything unfair. An interesting variation on this theme is the way he'll argue for something he doesn't necessarily believe in, just so the other viewpoint will be heard! Maddening? You bet!

Libra is the only sign whose symbol is neither human nor animal: rather it is the depiction of those scales of justice, and a better symbol couldn't be found to illustrate the seesaw effect that permeates just about everything in this man's life. Some days, he's up, some down. Then there comes that magical moment when he achieves perfect balance, utter harmony and contentment. If you're married to a Libra, you know what I mean. However, he's a refined and charming gentleman, so even when he is out of balance, he'll go to great pains not to ruffle the waters. He'd do almost anything to avoid a scene. He probably thinks that will make his scales go completely out of whack. Also, keep in mind that it upsets him terribly to think he's hurt your feelings. Chances are he'd rather see himself as a peacemaker, a Gentleman and a Scholar.

He could be quite comfortable on a country estate. His manse would be handsomely appointed, preferably with original works of art and a library replete with leatherbound first editions. Beauty soothes his nerves, helps to keep those scales somewhat balanced. Nothing undoes a Libran quite like confusion and disorder. And the sad part is, Libra—being the soul of kindness—is so loathe to tell you that he hates the fuchsia-and-chartreuse-striped wallpaper you picked out for the dining room that he'll forget it even bothers him, then wonder why he has indigestion. And you thought it was your cooking!

If you are married to a Libra, you're undoubtedly familiar with all the above. If you're just starting to date one of these Venusian gentlemen, you're probably more interested in the romantic prognosis—the decorating of dining rooms is still down the road a bit. Yes, what about *romance?* Well, to begin with, Libras wrote the book on the subject! You know, one of those leather-bound volumes that rests on the mahogany table by his fireplace. I kid you not! This man has more charm than the law should allow—and that smile.... No woman in her right mind could resist it. It's designed to melt any resistance you might have to him. It makes up for his inconsistencies. So, if you've been smitten by his charm, realize that even though it might take him a while to decide for sure if you're the one, he will decide, and when he does, he'll woo you with the kind of gentle finesse that will take your breath away. Rest assured, marriage is probably uppermost in his mind, and as you will soon find out, his tender style of lovemaking is the stuff that romance novels are made of.

You'll find this special brand of man drawn to work that is carried out in pleasant, creative surroundings. He could be anything from a diplomat to a trapeze artist. He would also do well as an art dealer, designer, musician or writer.

* * * * *

FAMOUS LIBRAN MEN

George Gershwin
F. Scott Fitzgerald
John Lennon
Marcello Mastroianni

WRITTEN IN THE STARS

STUNG BY LOVE

Will Susannah Dushay pay the price for sexy Scorpio Jake Taggart's revenge on her family in Ginna Gray's STING OF THE SCORPION, November's WRITTEN IN THE STARS?

Susannah only knew that Jake was her new employer and that he and his offer— *demand*—of marriage were difficult to resist. What would happen when she discovered the truth?

Find out in STING OF THE SCORPION by Ginna Gray... coming from Silhouette Romance this November. It's WRITTEN IN THE STARS!

Silhouette 🌹 *Romance*®

COMING NEXT MONTH

SILHOUETTE®
OFFICIAL SWEEPSTAKES RULES

NO PURCHASE NECESSARY

1. To enter, complete an Official Entry Form or 3"× 5" index card by hand-printing, in plain block letters, your complete name, address, phone number and age, and mailing it to: Silhouette Fashion A Whole New You Sweepstakes, P.O. Box 9056, Buffalo, NY 14269-9056.

   No responsibility is assumed for lost, late or misdirected mail. Entries must be sent separately with first class postage affixed, and be received no later than December 31, 1991 for eligibility.

2. Winners will be selected by D.L. Blair, Inc., an independent judging organization whose decisions are final, in random drawings to be held on January 30, 1992 in Blair, NE at 10:00 a.m. from among all eligible entries received.

3. The prizes to be awarded and their approximate retail values are as follows: Grand Prize — A brand-new Ford Explorer 4×4 plus a trip for two (2) to Hawaii, including round-trip air transportation, six (6) nights hotel accommodation, a $1,400 meal/spending money stipend and $2,000 cash toward a new fashion wardrobe (approximate value: $28,000) or $15,000 cash; two (2) Second Prizes — A trip to Hawaii, including round-trip air transportation, six (6) nights hotel accommodation, a $1,400 meal/spending money stipend and $2,000 cash toward a new fashion wardrobe (approximate value: $11,000) or $5,000 cash; three (3) Third Prizes — $2,000 cash toward a new fashion wardrobe. All prizes are valued in U.S. currency. Travel award air transportation is from the commercial airport nearest winner's home. Travel is subject to space and accommodation availability, and must be completed by June 30, 1993. Sweepstakes offer is open to residents of the U.S. and Canada who are 21 years of age or older as of December 31, 1991, except residents of Puerto Rico, employees and immediate family members of Torstar Corp., its affiliates, subsidiaries, and all agencies, entities and persons connected with the use, marketing, or conduct of this sweepstakes. All federal, state, provincial, municipal and local laws apply. Offer void wherever prohibited by law. Taxes and/or duties, applicable registration and licensing fees, are the sole responsibility of the winners. Any litigation within the province of Quebec respecting the conduct and awarding of a prize may be submitted to the Régie des loteries et courses du Québec. All prizes will be awarded; winners will be notified by mail. No substitution of prizes is permitted.

4. Potential winners must sign and return any required Affidavit of Eligibility/Release of Liability within 30 days of notification. In the event of noncompliance within this time period, the prize may be awarded to an alternate winner. Any prize or prize notification returned as undeliverable may result in the awarding of that prize to an alternate winner. By acceptance of their prize, winners consent to use of their names, photographs or their likenesses for purposes of advertising, trade and promotion on behalf of Torstar Corp. without further compensation. Canadian winners must correctly answer a time-limited arithmetical question in order to be awarded a prize.

5. For a list of winners (available after 3/31/92), send a separate stamped, self-addressed envelope to: Silhouette Fashion A Whole New You Sweepstakes, P.O. Box 4665, Blair, NE 68009.

PREMIUM OFFER TERMS

To receive your gift, complete the Offer Certificate according to directions. Be certain to enclose the required number of "Fashion A Whole New You" proofs of product purchase (which are found on the last page of every specially marked "Fashion A Whole New You" Silhouette or Harlequin romance novel). Requests must be received no later than December 31, 1991. Limit: four (4) gifts per name, family, group, organization or address. Items depicted are for illustrative purposes only and may not be exactly as shown. Please allow 6 to 8 weeks for receipt of order. Offer good while quantities of gifts last. In the event an ordered gift is no longer available, you will receive a free, previously unpublished Silhouette or Harlequin book for every proof of purchase you have submitted with your request, plus a refund of the postage and handling charge you have included. Offer good in the U.S. and Canada only.

SLFW·SWPR